SONG OF THE WITCH

WITCHES OF KEATING HOLLOW
BOOK SIXTEEN

DEANNA CHASE

Copyright © 2024 by Deanna Chase

Editing: Angie Ramey

Cover image: © Ravven

ISBN 978-1-965804-02-5

All rights reserved. No part of this publication may be reproduced, stored in, or introduced into a retrieval system, or transmitted in any form, or by any means (electronic, mechanical, photocopying, recording, or otherwise) without the prior written permission of both the copyright owner and the publisher of this book.

This book is a work of fiction. Names, characters, places, and incidents are products of the author's imagination or are used fictitiously. Any resemblance to actual events, locals, business establishments, or persons, living or dead, are entirely coincidental.

Bayou Moon Press, LLC

www.deannachase.com

Printed in the United States of America

ABOUT THIS BOOK

Spirit witch Sadie Lewis has never been a powerful witch. Her only talent is being able to feel other peoples' emotions, especially when she sings. It's what has kept her from pursuing a musical career. The idea of being overwhelmed with her empath ability while in the middle of a crowded concert venue is terrifying. But when the perfect deal comes around, she can't refuse. Only now she's been teamed up with King McGrath, a boy from her past who she hurt badly and it seems he might not ever forgive her.

Rocker King McGrath hasn't had the easiest life. After being kicked out of his home as a teen for his unusual abilities, trust is hard to come by. He's worked hard for every bit of success he'd managed, but his career is in a slump. When he finally lands a deal that gives him the control he's always craved, he learns he's now working with the one person he thought he'd never see again. Now he's moments from walking away from it all.

But when pain turns to healing and King finally starts to trust again, a curse wreaks havoc on the residents of Keating Hollow. Now it's up to Sadie and King to break it and restore the magical order to the special town they've both come to love. And just maybe they'll find a way to heal past wounds and get the happily-ever-after they both deserve.

CHAPTER 1

"Can you put this in the system?" Rhys asked, handing Sadie a handwritten phone order.

"Sure." Sadie wiped her hands on her apron and took the ticket. While on autopilot, she tapped on the point-of-sale screen and entered the order for the cheeseburger, fries, and a slice of apple pie. Her stomach tried to eat itself as she thought of the delicious apple crumble pie that was on the menu this month. When she finally got her break, she and a slice of that pie were going to have a moment.

Chuckling to herself, Sadie squinted at the name Rhys had scribbled at the bottom and then turned abruptly toward him. "Does this say King?"

He didn't look up from the notebook he was scribbling in as he said, "Yep."

Sadie let out a gasp and then quickly slapped her hand over her mouth.

Rhys glanced at her, his eyebrows raised. "I take it that means you two haven't cleared the air yet?"

Grimacing, she shook her head. A week ago, King

McGrath had walked back into her life, and then when he'd realized who she was, he'd walked right back out of it. That would have been bad enough, but they'd been on stage at the brewery in front of a large crowd, singing a song for the producer she'd hoped to work with when he'd abruptly walked out. Sadie had nearly died on the spot. It wasn't as though she was an experienced entertainer. After that, her performance had been shaky, and she'd been sure she'd blown her chance at a record deal.

She'd found out a few days later that she hadn't, in fact, blown it. But if she wanted the deal, she would have to record a duet with King McGrath. Her first instinct had been to say no. And she would have after the way King had acted, but she needed the money. Her tips at the Townsend Brewery weren't going to pay for the termite damage that had nearly destroyed the foundation and porch of the house she'd inherited from her mother. It was either sing with King or sell her mom's beloved house to some investor for pennies on the dollar before it was so bad it was condemned.

There had been no question. She'd signed the contract that afternoon.

But she still hadn't talked to King. Hadn't had a chance to clear the air. To explain why she'd ghosted him a decade ago.

"Excuse me!" a shiny teenager called from across the pub. The girl was waving her arms, acting like she was stranded on a deserted island and flagging down a rescue boat.

Sadie sighed and walked over to the table where six teenagers sat, each of them nursing glasses of iced tea. She pasted a smile on her face. "Are you ready to order?"

"Yes," the one who'd been waving at her said while giving her the stink eye. No doubt she thought Sadie had been ignoring them, but what did they expect? They'd sat down over two hours ago and had waved her off each time she'd come to ask if they needed anything other than refills on their iced teas.

"Shoot," Sadie said, pulling out her order pad.

"Two sides of fries with ranch and extra ketchup," the shiny one said.

Sadie repeated her order and then looked at the brunette next to her. "And you?"

"Oh, nothing," she said brightly. "We're sharing the fries."

"Two orders of fries for all of you. That's it?"

"Oh, we need refills," the shiny girl said, adding a bite to her tone.

"Right. I'll be back in a jiffy."

Sadie heard snickering as she left the table and wondered how, at twenty-seven, she'd become so uncool with the teenage crowd. Clearly she was already over the hill.

After she refilled the girls' tea and brought them their fries, she was busy drawing beer from a tap when she heard, "Order up!"

King's order was sitting under the warming lights, and she quickly boxed it up, adding extra condiments. Then she put the entire thing in the warming oven and waited impatiently for King to come for his lunch.

What should she say? Should she start with an apology and then try to explain what happened that summer all those years ago? But how could she when she didn't quite understand it herself? She slumped against the bar, praying that once the shock had worn off that King wasn't so angry anymore. That he could let the past go so they could move forward with their collaboration.

The door swung open and in walked King McGrath, the

dark-haired man with thick curls. The kind that made her want to run her fingers through his locks.

King's gaze instantly landed on hers. His expression was almost curious, but when he suddenly scowled, she knew he hadn't put anything behind them. Suddenly she was angry, too. Neither one of them were teenagers anymore. There was no reason to hold onto a grudge. Especially when she got butterflies just from looking at the handsome man. Sadie pressed a hand to her stomach and willed herself to settle. At this rate, she'd be yelling at him while aching for one of his kisses.

That would not do. That would not do at all.

"Oh. My. God. It's King McGrath!" the shiny girl cried as she clutched her hand to her chest.

All of her friends leaped out of their chairs and started to rush toward him, screaming his name.

King's eyes widened as a look of panic claimed his gorgeous features. He took a couple of steps back and nearly fell right over the hostess stand.

"It's kismet!" one of them cried as she tried to dodge one of the tables.

"Back off, Barbie!" the brunette ordered.

The five girls started to argue, each of them talking over each other.

King glanced at Sadie and the bag she was holding but then quickly shook his head and bolted for the door.

"Wait!" the shiny one cried as she scrambled to climb onto the table. "Don't you remember me?" She took a step toward the edge and continued. "We met last summer and—oof!"

The table collapsed, and the shiny girl flailed, putting her hands out in front of her to break her fall before landing with a thud on her right side.

Everyone was silent as the front door closed with a loud click.

"Penny?" the brunette asked quietly before running over to the girl who was clutching her arm and rocking back and forth.

"Oh, shit," Rhys said softly under his breath as he hurried out from behind the bar toward Penny and the brunette.

"What the hell happened?" Clay Garrison, the manager of the pub, asked.

Sadie jumped before she turned and found her boss standing right behind her. She hadn't even heard him come in from the back. "Those girls saw King McGrath and went all Beatlemania on him. When he bolted, that one climbed on the table. It collapsed, and then she fell. Hard."

"What does she think this is? A night club?" There was disgust in his tone as he grabbed his phone and made a call. "Drew?" he said almost immediately.

Sadie knew that had to be Drew Baker, the town's sheriff, who also happened to be Clay's brother-in-law.

"We need a transport to a healer. A customer got a little out of hand, and it looks like she hurt her arm pretty badly." Clay paused for a moment. "Yeah. Okay. See you in a few."

"You called the sheriff on her?" Sadie asked incredulously. "Hasn't she been punished enough?"

"I want it on the record that she was climbing on tables. That way if she or her parents decide to sue later, we have a record," Clay said calmly. Then he looked at the bag she was still holding. "What's that?"

"King's takeout order. He barely even made it in the door before the girls ran him off."

He nodded once and then walked over to Rhys. A few seconds later, Rhys was back, taking the food from her. "I'm going to run this over to King."

"I can do it," Sadie said quickly, reaching for the food again. That would be her perfect opportunity to apologize, and then hopefully tomorrow wouldn't be so awkward in the studio.

But Rhys shook his head as he took a few steps back. "Clay is going to need you to give your statement to Drew. I'll be right back."

Sadie watched him leave and then leaned both elbows on the bar and blew out a long, frustrated breath. Why was it so hard to get just one minute with King? Then she looked at the teenagers who were gathered around Penny and decided she had other things to worry about. Like cleaning up the broken ranch and ketchup bowls. Not to mention the splintered table.

It had already been a day, and it was barely lunch. She stared at the spot where she'd last seen King, and that flutter was back in her stomach from just thinking about him. She let out a groan. What was wrong with her? Straightening, she told herself to put the singer out of her mind as she went back to work.

CHAPTER 2

"Sadie!" Imogen Thane called as she waved from her table at Incantation Café. "Over here." The woman with dark blond hair had her curls piled on the top of her head and was dressed in jeans and a T-shirt with a *Married in the Redwoods* logo for her wedding coordinator business on the front.

"Tell me you already ordered my latte," Sadie begged as she plopped down onto one of the chairs across from her friend and blew out a long breath.

"It's on the way." Imogen gave her a sympathetic smile. "Rough day?"

"Very. The brewery was busier than usual. I think a lot of people are in town to see the Halloween decorations. But also, somehow the word got out that King McGrath is here, and a half-dozen girls were camped out there, just waiting to see if he would show up. They took up a large table all day and only ordered iced tea and two orders of fries in a three-hour time period. Do you have any idea how much tea teenagers can drink? Not only did I lose out on tips, but I'm fairly certain the Townsends lost money on that deal."

"Sounds awful." Imogen grimaced. "Neither Clay nor Rhys were bothered by them taking up a table?"

Sadie let out a humorless laugh. "No. It wasn't like people had to wait to sit down, so they just ignored them. Or they did until King actually walked in, and suddenly the girls tried to mob him. Not only did I *not* get to talk to him, but one of the girls climbed on one of the tables and then broke it *and* her arm. It was a complete shitshow."

"Her arm!" Imogen pressed her hand to her mouth and then shook her head. "Sorry to say, but she kinda deserved that, didn't she?"

"I'm not sure I'd go that far, but it is hard to feel sorry for her when she was climbing all over the furniture."

"Here you go, ladies," Hanna, the owner of the café, said as she placed two cups on the table along with two pastries. The gorgeous dark-skinned woman had her curls tucked into a high ponytail. She wore jeans, a red blouse, and a black apron that made her look like she'd just stepped out of a baking magazine. "Can I get you anything else?"

Sadie clutched her coffee as she gazed gratefully at Hanna. "You're a goddess."

Hanna chuckled. "I heard there was some excitement at the brewery today. Is everyone okay?"

"Mostly." Sadie took a long sip of her drink before she continued. "There's one tourist who is now sporting a cast on her arm that will likely be there for the next six weeks. I swear, people are crazy around celebrities."

"That's true," Hanna said, nodding. "But who were they stalking? Are Levi and Silas back in town?"

Sadie shrugged. "No idea. But if so, they weren't at the

brewery today. The mob was trying to get a glimpse of King McGrath."

"Seriously?" Hanna looked confused. "The guy Austin is working with to produce his comeback album?"

"Yep," Sadie said.

"But he only has like one hit song, right?" Hanna stared out the front window of her café as if she were looking for the man in question. "He can't be that famous, can he? And how do they even know where he is? This isn't LA or New York City."

"Oh, he's famous all right," Imogen explained. "I found a small but rabid community of fangirls online who've been following his every move for the last couple of years. As for how they find him, it appears some of them are very dedicated to scouring the entire internet for any hint of a sighting. All it takes is one Tweet or TikTok, and suddenly their entire message board knows where he is."

"Good goddess. That sounds miserable. I'd never want to be famous." Hanna made a face. "Did King make it out all right?"

"Yeah," Sadie said with a sigh. "He was just there to pick up food, but he couldn't even make it to the counter. He walked in, saw the mob of teenagers, and split. Rhys ended up taking the order over to Austin's studio."

"That's too bad that you didn't get to talk to him," Imogen said, her eyes full of sympathy.

"I really was hoping it would be my chance before we have to meet up tomorrow." After the debacle when King had walked out on Sadie while they were singing at the brewery, she'd confided in Imogen and had confessed their history. Imogen was the one who'd encouraged her to just try to talk it out with King.

And Sadie had tried. Before they'd ever gotten on that stage a week ago, King had been sweet and flirty with her. They'd ended up exchanging numbers even though they hadn't even recognized each other. Because she had his number, she'd called him and texted, but he hadn't answered. Honestly, Sadie didn't even blame him. Not really. She had walked out of his life a decade ago without even saying goodbye. If the situation had been reversed, she'd likely still be angry, too. It probably didn't help that she hadn't even recognized him at first. But to be fair, he hadn't recognized her either. They'd both been skinny teenagers back then, and she'd known King as Kevin, his given name, so she thought she should be forgiven for the slight. Though she wasn't sure what *his* excuse was. She'd always used the name Sadie.

"That sucks." Imogen reached across the table and squeezed Sadie's hand. "I know you really wanted to smooth things over with him. But you'll see him at the studio tomorrow, right?"

Sadie slumped back in her chair, feeling defeated. "Sure. But talk about awkward. What am I supposed to do? Grovel right there in front of Austin Steele, the record producer?"

Hanna blinked at Sadie and then cleared her throat. "I know it's none of my business, but did something happen between you and King last week? You're not fighting already, are you?"

"Not last week," Sadie said. "A decade ago. We have history. But we were just kids then, and we didn't even recognize each other until we were on stage singing."

Hanna let out a low whistle. "That is complicated. And now you have to work together?"

"Only if King shows up tomorrow," Sadie said, not at all

sure he would. Austin had seemed... unsure, but he'd said he'd work on him.

"I'm sure he will," Hanna said as she pointed her chin at something outside.

Sadie turned and spotted King standing outside the café, staring right at her. Their gazes held for a long moment. Sadie stood abruptly and headed for the door, intending to go talk to him. But before she could make it outside, King scowled and then walked briskly away.

"Dammit," Sadie muttered to herself as she hurried outside. "King! Wait, I want to apologize!"

But King didn't look back at her as he quickly rounded a corner with another man who was about a head taller than him.

Defeated, Sadie slowly walked back into the café and took her seat.

"Brutal," Hanna muttered.

Imogen made a sound of agreement.

"What am I going to do?" Sadie asked the two women. "This contract is what is going to save my mom's house. If I can't pay for the repairs, I could end up homeless soon."

"First, Austin won't drop you from your contract because King is being difficult," Imogen said, her voice full of conviction. "Second, you're not going to be homeless. We'll figure out a way to get you the money for repairs even if we have to do a town fundraiser."

Sadie groaned. "I can't take a handout like that. Maybe I can find another bank that will give me a loan. If I can find a way to make my income-to-debt ratio a little more bank friendly, I think maybe they'd do it."

Hanna bit her bottom lip as though studying the problem. "You can always help out here or at the winery for extra money if you need to. Candy and I could definitely use the help, and I know my parents are looking for some help with all the events they are booking now."

"Really?" Sadie asked, feeling a little more hopeful. She didn't relish the thought of working seven days a week, but she'd do it if she had to. "Thanks, Hanna. I appreciate that."

"No problem. Rhys is always talking about what a hard worker you are. If I had my way, we'd have stolen you a long time ago, but I know we can't compete with the tips you must get at the brewery." Hanna was married to Rhys, the assistant manager at the pub, and she came in regularly. She was also best friends with Abby Townsend, so Sadie had known her for years. Hanna was good people, and Sadie really did appreciate her offer.

"Yeah," Sadie said, forcing herself to chuckle. "I could never leave the Townsends. They're like family after all these years. But I'll let you know if the music thing falls through."

Hanna squeezed her shoulder as she nodded and then hurried back to the counter to help her cousin Candy, who was getting swamped by a fresh wave of customers.

Sadie grabbed her coffee cake and her cup. "Are you ready for that hike? I could use a little peace and quiet."

"Absolutely." Imogen gathered her items and the pair of them exited the café and walked over to Sadie's red Toyota Camry that was parked a few stores down in front of A Spoonful of Magic.

"Thanks for coming with me," Sadie said as she backed out of the space. "I love hiking, but going alone always feels a little risky."

"Of course. You know I'm always up for stretching my legs. Besides, it's a good way to get a little girl time in after dealing with bridezillas all day." She winked, letting Sadie know she was just teasing. The truth was that Imogen loved her job. And she didn't just coordinate weddings. She planned all kinds of parties and had become the go-to event coordinator in Keating Hollow in just a few short months.

They smiled at each other. Imogen was pretty new in town, having only moved there after her sister, Harlow Thane, the famous ghost hunter, had relocated to Keating Hollow after her TV show had ended. Imogen and Sadie had become fast friends after Imogen had worked on Sadie's cousin's wedding a few months back.

It didn't take long for them to reach the trailhead that was just a few miles outside of downtown.

"Looks like we're not the only ones interested in seeing the falls this afternoon," Imogen said as she jumped out of the car.

"Huh." Sadie eyed the black SUV that was taking up two spots and then rolled her eyes. "Looks like they could use parking lessons."

The pair of them laughed as they tugged their sweatshirts on, grabbed their water bottles, and then hit the trail. The afternoon sun was already low in the sky, and if they wanted to reach the falls and get back before nightfall, they were going to need to book it. They didn't speak much as they hurried along the trail, and only when they heard the falls did Sadie say, "Oh, good. We're almost there."

She sped up to round a curve in the trail, and as soon as she passed a large redwood, she ran smack into someone. "Oof!"

"What the hell?" the man barked. "Watch where you're—"

Their eyes met, and the man, King McGrath, suddenly stopped talking.

They both froze.

"Kevin?" Sadie said, automatically using the name he'd given her all those years ago. "What are you doing here?"

He took a step back, putting space between them. "Are you following me?"

"What?" Sadie was taken aback by his accusation.

"First you came after me at the café, and now you're here. What else would you call it?"

Sadie blinked at him. "The café? You were the one who stopped to stare at me. I was just trying to talk to you, but I went right back inside after you ran off. How was that following you?"

"You know I'm not interested in— You know what? Never mind." He gestured to a man behind him that she hadn't noticed. It was the taller man he'd been with when she'd seen him at the café. "Let's go Briggs," King said. "I don't need this. Not today." He moved past her, but then paused and said, "The name is King, not Kevin."

Briggs mouthed *sorry* as he followed King back down the trail.

Sadie stared at them, open-mouthed.

"Hey," Imogen said gently. "You okay?"

"Huh?" Sadie jerked her head as she turned and look at her friend. "Oh. Sorry. Yeah. It's just… That was weird, right?"

"Definitely." Imogen slipped her arm through Sadie's and said, "Let's just go see the waterfall so we can turn back before it gets dark."

Sadie nodded absently and let her friend lead her down the rest of the trail. But her mind was a million miles away as she tried to reconcile the man who'd just stalked off with the boy she'd met on the beach in Westhaven all those years ago.

CHAPTER 3

King paced the living room of his friend's house and ran his hand through his short curls. What in the world was wrong with him? Why was he letting Sadie Lewis get under his skin? It had been years since he'd thought of the girl he'd met on the beach when he was just seventeen and barely getting by after his parents had kicked him out.

"Hey," Briggs said, walking into the room with his hair wet from his shower. "I ordered pizza, and I'll grab some beer after I pick it up. Any special requests?"

"Can we head to LA and get it there?" King asked, flopping down on the couch. "Maybe if we flee, I can convince Austin to record this album down there."

"You know he sold his studio down there and moved all his operations here, right?" Briggs tugged a sweatshirt on and then covered his hair with a ball cap. "I doubt he'd be happy about renting space just because you don't want to be in the same room with a girl you had a crush on a decade ago."

King glared at his friend. "You don't know what you're talking about."

Briggs shrugged. "Maybe not, but I know enough to understand that you're being pretty dramatic about a girl you haven't talked about in years. If she bothers you that much, just tell Austin you don't want to do the duet with her. What's the worst he can say, no? If it's you or her, he's going to pick you. You're the one with the hit song, remember?"

"Yeah. I guess." King stared past Briggs, trying to block out the gorgeous woman's face. He still didn't understand how he hadn't recognized her the week before at the pub until they'd started singing together. Her eyes had haunted him for many years. Not to mention that thick, dark blond hair of hers. Why hadn't he recognized her dark eyes? The rest of her… Well, she'd grown up quite a bit in the last ten years.

"I'll be back with pizza and beer. Don't make any decisions until I get back," Briggs said.

King waved him off. He wasn't going to call Austin. King wasn't an idiot. Not only was he not going to make waves with Austin, the one producer who'd agreed to let King record his music his way, but he also knew that Sadie had the voice of an angel. She was absolutely perfect for the duet. He let out a groan and slumped down into the couch with his eyes closed.

The cool breeze off the ocean and the scent of the saltwater came rushing back. There he was, seventeen again, holding hands with Sadie as they walked under the moonlight along the shore. He'd been so nervous the first time he'd reached for her hand, but when she'd slipped her fingers through his and smiled at him, he'd felt his heart swell. The darkness that had been clinging to him dissipated. And finally, after what felt like a lifetime of rejection, King had felt wanted. Alive. Like his life finally made sense.

There was something about the quiet girl that had spoken to him the first time they'd met. He'd just felt... right. Like she was a kindred spirit.

"I talked to the manager at Westie's," King had said to her, his voice full of excitement. "He said we could go on tomorrow night as the pre-opener. We won't get paid, but we would get a portion of the tips. What do you think?"

Sadie glanced at him, her eyes wide as she bit down on her lower lip. "Tomorrow night?"

He squeezed her hand, knowing she was a ball of nerves. He was too. It would be the first time he'd sung live other than busking down at the pier. They'd be on stage, under the lights, and they were expected to start warming up the audience. "You can do it. You're a natural."

"I don't know about that," she said with a nervous laugh. "I've never done anything like that before. What if I freeze in front of everyone?"

King stopped and held both of her hands in his and met her gaze. "You won't freeze, but if you do, I'll be right there. You just focus on me, and we'll sing just like we did in that cove over there the night we met." He pointed to the outcropping of rocks that hid a small cove next to the beach.

Sadie glanced over at the place he'd come to think of as theirs. A tiny hint of a smile claimed her lips.

"Come on," he said, tugging her gently toward the cove.

"Are you trying to get me alone, Kevin?" she'd asked with that tinkling laugh that he now heard in his dreams.

"What gave it away?" he asked with a wink and then

laughed when she broke out into a run toward their spot. He sprinted after her, and by the time they'd rounded the rock that shielded the entrance to the little cove, they were both out of breath.

Sadie collapsed onto the sand and then reached out, taking his hand and tugging him down after her. He landed half on top of her and half on the sand, their lips just a couple inches apart.

"Sadie," he whispered, staring at her pink lips, desperate to kiss her. He'd been dying to press his lips to hers since the first day they'd met, but he hadn't managed to work up the nerve. But now...

"Kevin," she whispered back as her eyes fluttered closed, and she lightly pressed her palm to his cheek. When her tongue darted out, moistening her lips, he knew it was now or never.

The world stopped. He heard nothing but the crash of the waves and the soft sounds of her breath as he bent his head and very lightly kissed her.

Sadie arched up slightly, increasing the pressure of their lips as she let out a small sigh. The sound of that little noise, along with the scent of the sea-salted air, was burned into his memories. Still to this day, he sometimes woke up hearing that sigh, convinced he was right back there at that beach with the only girl he'd ever wanted still wrapped in his arms.

King's eyes popped open as his hand flew to his mouth. His lips tingled as if he'd actually just been kissing Sadie Lewis instead of only remembering the last night before she'd ghosted him by leaving town without even so much as a goodbye.

His heart ached just below his breastbone like it always

did when he thought of her. Unconsciously, he rubbed at the spot and wondered if Briggs had been onto something. Maybe he should tell Austin the duet wasn't going to work after all. How was he going to survive being in the same room with her if his chest kept aching when he was just thinking about her?

His phone trilled, startling him out of his thoughts. King glanced down at the screen and scowled when he saw the caller. Normally he'd ignore it and let the call go to voice mail, but he was in a mood, and unleashing his frustration on Cindy McGrath seemed like the perfect thing to do.

"Mother," he said coolly into the phone.

"Oh, Kevin," she said, her tone overly sweet. "I finally managed to get you on the phone. You must be really busy. What's it been? Six months since I talked to you?"

Try eighteen, he thought bitterly. And that was only because he'd had a hit song earlier that year and she'd tried to cash in. Then and only then had his mother decided he was worth talking to. He wouldn't have even answered now, except she'd been calling for a couple of weeks and he knew she wouldn't stop until she got him on the line. "Something like that," he said. "What do you need?"

"Now, Kevin. Don't be like that. I just called to see how you are."

King didn't buy it for a second. His mother only ever called when she wanted something. "It's King now," he told her for the hundredth time.

"Right." She chuckled softly. "It's just so hard for me to remember. You'll always be Kevin to me. My baby."

He wanted to scream at her. Or throw something at the television sitting in front of him. King had never been more than an afterthought unless his magic was flaring up. Then they'd thought he was a major nuisance. Like it was his fault he couldn't control his magic when he was just six years old.

"What did you call for, Mother?" he asked, not bothering to hide the irritation in his tone.

She sighed heavily. "Can't a mother call to just check on her son?"

That would be great, except they both knew that wasn't why she called. He didn't respond, waiting for her to get to the point.

"Fine. I do need something, but I'm sure it's just pocket change to you. I need to buy a new car."

He snorted out a humorless laugh. "What's wrong with your old one?"

"Your father had a minor fender bender, and we're told it's not worth it to fix it."

He very much doubted her story. Her SUV was only a couple of years old. If it was a minor fender bender, they'd just pound out the dents and get on with it. "How much?"

This time she let out a nervous giggle. "Well, there's this cute little Lexus that just rolled onto the lot."

"You want money for a brand new Lexus?" he asked incredulously. What was that? Fifty grand at least? But knowing his mother, she'd be looking at something that was top of the line.

"You want your mother to be safe, right? Lexus has the highest rated safety features," she said as if she were being completely reasonable.

"You can get a Toyota. Used. I'll transfer some money tonight, but don't ask for more. Contrary to what you think, I'm not printing money over here. Got it?"

"But, Kevin—"

"Good night, Mother." He ended the call and put her number on ignore. He went into his app, sent his mother enough money for a decent used car, and then threw his phone across the room. It crashed against the wall before clattering to the hardwood floors and bouncing twice. Not caring if he'd shattered it, he strode into the kitchen and angrily grabbed the last beer out of the fridge. After he downed half of it, he looked at the bottle and said, "Briggs better hurry. I'm gonna need another six pack or two."

Just as he drained the last of the beer, he heard Briggs open the front door and call, "Pizza!"

Without a word, King walked into the living room, took the case of beer from his friend, and opened it right there on the coffee table. He used the bottle opener he'd brought with him to uncap two of them. And then raising both, he said, "To all the mothers who should have never had kids."

Briggs raised both eyebrows. "You talked to Cindy?"

"Yup." King tilted one of the bottles up and drained a good third before he let up.

His friend took the other open bottle, clinked it to King's, and said, "To found family."

King looked up at his friend and felt a little bit of the ache in his chest ease. As he raised his bottle again, he choked out, "To found family."

They each took a swig before Briggs put his arm around King's shoulders and steered him toward the kitchen. "Come on. We have pizza to eat."

King nodded and let his friend guide him until he deposited him in a chair at the table. Before he knew it, Briggs had piled his plate with pizza, gotten him another beer, and was back in his chair, diving into the cheesy goodness.

Following his friend's lead, King focused on the pizza and did his best to push Cindy McGrath from his mind. It was just too bad that when he cleared his head, Sadie crept right back in. He let out a groan and then took a vicious bite of the pizza. It was going to be a long night.

CHAPTER 4

Sadie Lewis sat in the recording studio and wiped at her brow. The lights were beating down on her, but they weren't the only thing making her sweat. King McGrath sat with Austin, staring at her through the glass from the adjoining room.

"King?" Austin Steel, the music producer said into his microphone. "Can you join Sadie in the recording booth?"

"But she's not done with her verses," King said.

"I know. I want to try it with you both singing the chorus and then doing some voice layering."

"But that's not how the song is written," King argued.

"You're right," Austin said, sounding impatient. "But we're going to try it anyway."

King scowled but got up and did as Austin said without another word. The door slammed shut behind him as he walked into the booth, and the two of them stared at each other for a long moment.

Sadie swallowed the lump in her throat as she waited to see what he'd do.

Finally he sighed, grabbed the acoustic guitar from the stand next to Sadie, and sat on a stool as he turned his attention to Austin. "You've got me in here. Now what do you want?"

Austin rolled his eyes. "Obviously I want you to sing with Sadie. Try it with her singing the first verse, you both sing the chorus, and then you come in on the second verse. If it works, we'll do some voice layering on the bridge. Understand?"

"Sure," King said, focusing on his guitar.

"Sadie?" Austin asked.

She cleared her throat, praying she didn't look like she wanted to bolt from the room. Ever since she'd gotten there, King had either been hostile or had ignored her completely. It made for a tension-filled session. Sadie wondered if she should just walk out. Was a record deal worth putting herself through the torture of dealing with a hostile rock star? But if she did, that would be the second time in her life she'd walked out on King, and that just wasn't something she could bear. Sadie lifted her head high and said, "Yeah, I'm ready."

The music started, and Austin pointed at Sadie, giving her the signal to start recording.

The music washed over her and as always, the notes seemed to seep right into her very soul. Music had always had a hold on her, and when she sang, it was the only time she felt completely whole.

It was also when her empath ability kicked in, and she could sense other people's emotions. Immediately, she was overwhelmed with an onslaught of King's emotions. Anger heated her skin, and it was all she could do to get her verse out before her throat closed from the intensity of it all.

As soon as her notes faded away, she opened her eyes and stared at the man sitting across from her. His gaze was locked on her, and Sadie felt herself shrinking into herself, wishing the floor would just open up and swallow her whole. How in the hell was she going to endure recording an entire song with a man who hated her for something that had happened a decade ago?

But as soon as she started in on the chorus and King's voice joined hers, the anger started to dissipate. And underneath all that emotion, she felt pain that was buried in a deep-seated wound, and she couldn't help but wonder if her actions all those years ago had contributed to the beautiful man's trauma.

King raised his gaze to hers and together they finished singing the chorus, their voices melding into the beautiful melody. Magic crackled around them as all the pain and emotion faded away, replaced by something that made her feel alive and like everything was just *right*. It was as if the universe had conspired to bring them together to sing this song in this place at that very moment.

Sadie stared into King's eyes and got lost in the blue sea that was reflected back at her, and she poured every ounce of herself into the song. She was lit up from the inside, feeling more alive than she ever had before.

Memories of her time with King all those years ago rushed in. The two of them on the beach. King singing a song he'd written. Them walking hand and hand under the moonlight and sharing secrets neither had ever shared with another. They'd been young, not quite eighteen, and both were struggling with difficult family situations. But she'd known instantly that they'd crossed paths for a reason. It was a connection she'd never had before and hadn't had since.

And one she'd missed every day of her life after her dad had shown up and abruptly unrooted her to Salem without any warning.

The song ended with Sadie and King staring at each other. The magic still crackled around them like electricity, and Sadie couldn't help the small smile that claimed her lips. "Did you feel that?"

He raised one eyebrow in question.

"We just made something special, King. I can feel it in my bones."

His eyes suddenly narrowed, and he stood abruptly, nearly knocking his chair over before he stormed out of the booth.

"King?" Austin called, his voice booming over the intercom. "Where are you going?"

The beautiful man with the deep blue eyes and a voice like an angel didn't respond as he disappeared through another door.

Sadie met Austin's gaze through the glass and said, "I think that went well, don't you?"

Austin let out a loud laugh and shook his head. Then he pointed at the door and said, "Go find him and bring him back. We still have work to do."

"Me?" she asked, pressing a hand to her chest. "I'm pretty sure he left because of me. Maybe we just need to let him clear his head."

He frowned. "He's been trying to work through this for a week now. After what I just witnessed, it's clear no amount of time is going to help until you two clear the air."

"And if we can't?" Sadie asked, staring at the door where King had disappeared. Every time she'd tried to talk to him

SONG OF THE WITCH

this week, he'd run from her. It didn't look like he was interested in clearing anything up between them.

"You can and you will," he said gently. "And it's not because of the contracts you both signed. It's because of what just happened when you two were singing. That's something very rare, and all three of us know it. So go. Work it out. I'll be here when you're both ready to finish this song."

Sadie's limbs felt like lead as she stood and forced herself to follow King while being fully prepared for him to bolt again. He wasn't hard to find. Once she stepped outside into the parking lot that was behind the building, she found King pacing and holding an unlit cigarette between his fingers. Sadie slowly walked over to him and said, "Do you need a light?"

He paused and glanced over at her. "I don't smoke."

Her gaze traveled to the cigarette between his thumb and forefinger.

"Okay, I used to snoke when I was a dumb teenager. Holding one helps me settle when I'm agitated."

"Understandable." Sadie's grandmother used to smoke. She'd watched her hold her cigarettes in exactly the same way when she had something on her mind. "Austin sent me out here to clear the air."

He just nodded.

Sadie swallowed the lump in her throat and decided to dive in instead of giving him another chance to bolt. "I'm sorry for the way I left Westhaven. I should have told you. Should have said goodbye. I just... couldn't."

"Couldn't?" he asked with a bite in his tone. "Why is that, Sadie? Was it just too much trouble? Or were you afraid I was so pathetic that I'd beg you to stay?"

"What?" she asked, startled by what appeared to be self-loathing in his tone. "No. That wasn't it at all." She stared at his hand that was holding the cigarette and desperately wished she had one of her own just to have something else to focus on.

"Then tell me," he demanded, sounding both anguished and angry. "Do you have any idea what it was like waiting for you at Westies only to have you not show up? And then when I called, your phone was disconnected. You couldn't have made it any plainer that you didn't want to see or talk to me."

Tears burned Sadie's eyes, and she blinked rapidly to fight them back. "Kevin, I—"

"It's King now."

"Right. Sorry." Her throat was tight as her anxiety shot through the roof. She wasn't proud of the way she'd handled things back then, but she had the opportunity to at least explain herself now. "When I got back to my grandma's that night we met on the beach, my father was there."

"Your father?" He frowned. "The one who abandoned you and your mom when you were six?"

Sadie nodded, surprised he'd remembered that detail. "Yeah. The one and only. He came with a court order giving him custody, and I had no choice but to go to Salem with him. My grandmother and I begged him to let me stay, but he said if I didn't go, he'd get the authorities involved. He threatened my grandmother by saying he'd file a complaint and drag her through the courts if she let me stay there. It was really combative and ugly, and I just…" She shook her head. "I didn't know what to do."

King was frozen as he took in her confession. "So your dad came in and yanked you away from your grandmother just three months after you'd lost your mom?"

"Yeah. That's pretty much it." Sadie's mom had died just before her seventeenth birthday. She been devastated. Not only had Steph Lewis been her mother, but she'd been her best friend, too. Her grandmother had visited them often, and the three were extremely close. She'd been there when Sadie's mom had passed, and not long after, she'd packed Sadie up and taken her to Westhaven, the beach town where she'd lived her entire life. While Sadie hadn't wanted to leave Keating Hollow, she'd wanted to be with her grandmother more.

"Sadie," King said softly.

She cleared the tears in her eyes and looked up at him. "Yeah?"

King stuffed the cigarette into his pocket and swiftly crossed the distance between them and wrapped her in his arms.

Sadie melted into him, clutching his shirt as tears streamed silently down her face. She hadn't wanted to cry. Hadn't wanted to have a meltdown while apologizing for ghosting him. But that was one of the reasons she hadn't had the courage to go see him before she'd left Westhaven. "King, I didn't find you before we left because I was afraid I'd beg you to run away with me."

He let out a chuckle that made his entire body vibrate. "You wouldn't have had to beg."

"I know. But we were just kids with nothing. I couldn't let you leave your foster home. Not after you'd finally found a decent one. If we'd run off, who knows where we'd be now?" She buried her face into his chest until her tears stopped and then finally pulled away, wiping at her cheeks. "I'm sorry. I didn't mean to make this all about me."

He stuffed his hands into his jeans pockets and hunched

his shoulders, suddenly looking uncomfortable. "Thank you for telling me. But for the record, I think if we had bolted, we'd probably be international rock stars by now." His lips twitched up into a twisted smile. "I heard there was a scout in the audience at Westies that night."

"He didn't sign you on the spot?" she asked, already thinking the guy must have been an idiot. King McGrath had a voice like no other.

He chuckled. "Hard to sign someone who no-shows on a gig."

"Wait. You didn't show up either?"

"Oh, I did," he said. "But when you didn't show up, I took off looking for you. I was worried. I went to your grandmother's house, but no one answered. I was too upset to play."

Sadie's heart ached for what she'd put him through. If she'd just had the courage to tell him, or even leave him a voice mail or text, he wouldn't have been worried about her safety at least. She cleared her throat. "My grandmother moved to Salem with us. She died five months later. The minute I graduated from high school I came back here to Keating Hollow to my mother's house."

"I'm sorry, Sadie. I know how much you loved her."

She nodded. "I did."

"But you never came back to Westhaven?" he asked.

"No," she said with a small shake of her head. "That was a rough time, and it was all I could do to keep my head above water."

"Understandable." He reached out and squeezed her hand briefly before dropping it and stepping back again. They were silent for a long moment before he said, "We should probably get back inside."

"Sure." But Sadie didn't move.

"What is it?" he asked.

"Are we okay? I mean, okay enough to work together, because that song—"

King held his hand up, stopping her. "We're recording that song. No doubt about it. I'll tell you what…"

She raised one eyebrow, waiting for him to continue.

"How about we let the past go and just focus on the future?" he asked.

"That sounds perfect." Sadie smiled, and it felt like she was beaming. But then she sobered. "There's just one thing I have to know."

"If it has to do with the contract or payment or anything like that, you'll have to talk to Austin. He has people who handle that stuff."

"No, it's not that." She had to refrain from rolling her eyes. "I need to know how it is you have all those memories from Westhaven, but you didn't recognize me earlier in the evening last week."

"You didn't recognize me either," he countered.

"That's because you have a new name and about another fifty pounds of muscle." Sadie let her gaze run the length of him before she looked him in the eye again. "You're like a Greek god now. Back then…" She shrugged one shoulder. "You were a skinny teenager, not… this."

"I could say the same about you," he said, not bothering to hide that he was checking her out.

"But I didn't change my name," she said, accusation in her tone.

"True, but I always think of you as Kitty, so it took me a minute to make the connection."

Sadie clasped her hand over her heart that was trying to

pound right out of her chest. She could still hear her mother call up the stairs, *Kitty! Dinner.*

"Oh hell," she said. "Are you trying to break me?" Kitty was the nickname that her mother had given her when she was still a toddler.

"Not today," he said with a smirk before adding, "Come on. Austin is waiting." He wrapped an arm around her shoulders and led her back inside.

CHAPTER 5

"I'm screwed." King picked at his dinner. The lobster mac and cheese had seemed like a great idea when he'd ordered it, but now he hardly had an appetite at all.

"About what?" Briggs asked and shoveled his crab fettuccini into his mouth.

"About what?" King echoed with a sardonic laugh. "You mean *who*, don't you?"

Briggs put his fork down and stared at his friend. "Why? Austin said things went pretty smoothly after this first session. He said you two seemed to have talked things out. That's good, right?"

It wasn't a surprise that Austin had told Briggs about the session. His friend and foster brother was the entire reason that Austin even knew about King in the first place. While King had always known he wanted to be a performer, Briggs had been more interested in the technical side. Right after they'd graduated from high school and been kicked out of their foster home, the pair had taken off for LA. They both had worked on a landscaping crew in Hollywood Hills to make money while doing whatever they could to break into their chosen fields. For King, that was singing. But Briggs had taken online classes for audio engineering and eventually found a job with Austin at his LA studio. When Austin closed shop and moved to Keating Hollow, Briggs had gone with him.

"Yeah. Sure. But you know how I feel about her. It's going to be torture doing the promo when my head is a freakin' mess." Briggs had been there since the very beginning. He knew just how hurt and upset King had been when Sadie had disappeared.

"Feel about her?" Briggs raised both eyebrows. *"Feel,* not felt?"

"That's why I'm screwed." King sat back in his chair, ignoring his food. "Singing with her… It all just came rushing back. This is going to sound insane, but she and I, we just fit. I've never felt a connection like that before, and if it doesn't work out, what then? I'm going to be haunted by that song forever."

"If what doesn't work out?" Briggs asked, studying his friend. "Your singing partnership or something more?"

King groaned. "Both, I guess."

"Oh boy." Briggs placed his elbows on the table and leaned in. "King, you have got to stop romanticizing how you feel about this girl. I'm not trying to be a dick, but you only knew her for a few months and that was ten years ago. You two barely even know each other."

He was wrong. King knew he was just trying to help, but that summer when he'd spent most of his nights with Sadie on the beach, he'd told her things about himself that he'd never told anyone before. And she'd shared her grief and hopes and fears for the future with him. They had a bond. It wasn't romanticized. It just *was*. "I hear you, brother. But it's not what you think."

Briggs's lips curved into a hint of a smile. "And what do I think?"

"That I've lost my mind."

He cackled. "That's true. I do think that. But all I'm trying to do is keep you grounded. When this song makes it big, and it will, then you two will be linked forever, and there will be a lot of promos. Your life will be hell if you turn it romantic and everything goes to shit. You do know that, right?"

King nodded. His friend was right. With the way he felt about her, if they did get together and then broke up, he didn't know how he'd recover from that. "So you're saying it's best to keep it professional."

"I hate to be that person, but yeah. This song and this album are what's going to solidify your career. Effing it up because you can't keep it in your pants would be just about the most cliché thing you could do."

"How boring would that be?" King said with a chuckle, trying to make light of everything. The truth was, King didn't really think it mattered if he slept with Sadie or not when it came to why or how they could mess this up. What he felt for her transcended the physical. And what he needed from her was a whole lot more than a night in the sack.

"Just try not to get too wrapped up in her," Briggs added. "Let's just focus on getting this record made and out in the world, and then maybe you two can see where this thing between you goes if you're still into it."

Easier said than done when all King wanted to do was find out where she lived and drive over to her house. But he just nodded, knowing that Briggs was right. What he needed to do was stay away from her and concentrate on work. At least until the record was released and they started their promo. By then, maybe all these feelings that had been stirred up would just go back into hibernation.

One could only hope.

A burning sensation started at the base of King's spine, making him jerk his head up. A trio of three young women who were all wearing jeans and cropped tank tops were headed straight for his table.

"Damn," Briggs muttered, waving down the waiter. "I'd hoped that being in Keating Hollow would have meant you had a little peace from all this."

King had hoped the same thing. It wasn't as if he was so famous that people recognized him everywhere. Hardly. However, there was a small but determined group of young women who'd taken to tracking him down everywhere he went. He'd thought moving to Keating Hollow would stop that, but it had only made it worse. It wasn't as if there were many places to hide in the tiny town.

The petite redhead who was making a beeline for him flashed a flirty smile, and suddenly her thoughts popped into King's mind. *There he is! Oh my effing goddess, he's hot. What I wouldn't do to get him naked.*

It took everything he had not to recoil from her and her friends, one of which was already recording him on her phone.

"Oh my gosh, King McGrath," the redhead gushed and then went on to proclaim, "I'm your biggest fan. Do you mind if we get a photo?" She was already handing her phone to the woman who wasn't recording the interaction.

"Sure," he said, doing his best to be gracious. He knew the drill. Being kind didn't cost him anything but a little inconvenience. But if he did anything to appear rude and it was caught on camera, then that was what would go viral. It wasn't worth the fallout just because his skin was crawling from hearing her thoughts.

King's telepathic ability was a major inconvenience. He hated being able to read minds. Not only was it intrusive, but he just didn't want to know people's private thoughts. He was happier being in the dark. At least he'd learned how to control it around most people. It was only when someone was overly excited or really worked up when thoughts assaulted his mind now.

Like this woman hanging all over him. She was dying to kiss him and had a running fantasy of the two of them in a shower together. It was all he could do not to just push her away. Instead, he pasted a smile on his face and leaned in so that their heads were nearly touching as her friend took the photo.

When he started to pull back, the woman clutched at him.

"Wait! Would you do me a favor?" she asked, giving him an innocent smile, all while picturing him naked.

"I'm sorry." King waved at Briggs, who was now holding two takeout boxes. "We're already late for an engagement. We're going to have to—"

"It'll just take two seconds. See, I'm an influencer with a large following, and I specialize in highlighting up-and-coming musicians."

That part appeared to be true at least, considering a screenshot of her IG had just flashed in her mind.

"And one of the running jokes is that I always manage to get a kiss from my favorites. I promised my followers that if I ever met you, I'd do my best to get a kiss right here." She pointed to her cheek and tapped it with a blood-red nail.

King felt like he was trapped. If he said no, he'd look like a jerk. But if he said yes, he'd need to bleach his lips later to stop the heebie-jeebies from taking over.

"Kiss! Kiss! Kiss!" the two other women started chanting.

"Yeah, okay." King leaned down and moved in to peck her cheek, but just before he made the connection, the woman turned her head and full-on assaulted his lips with her own.

Her two friends cheered.

King froze and then felt himself being pulled away.

The minute they were outside, Briggs started to rant about consent, and crazy fans, and how sorry he was that he hadn't acted sooner. "We're going to have to come up with a game plan so that doesn't happen to you again. The nerve!" he said as he opened the SUV door for King. "The only reason I didn't cuss them out was because of the video."

Once Briggs was in the driver's seat, King finally wiped his mouth and said, "Thank you for showing restraint. It's not worth whatever media it would have created."

"It's still not right. I could tell the minute the redhead touched you that you wanted to be anywhere but there." Briggs sped down the street, his driving more aggressive than usual.

"She had a porn track in her head of what she wanted to do with me," King said, feeling miserable. Was this what he had to look forward to for the rest of his life just because he wanted to make music?

Briggs glanced over at him. "Seriously?"

"Seriously. Now I need a shower."

"We definitely need to get a PR person, stat," Briggs said.

King just nodded as he leaned back into the seat and tried his best to put the entire thing out of his mind.

CHAPTER 6

"There you are," Melissa, Sadie's next-door neighbor and best friend in the world, said as Sadie climbed the stairs to her porch. Melissa had been sitting on the porch swing, waiting for her.

"Hey!" Sadie ran over to her and gave her a hug. "When did you get back in town?"

"Just about an hour ago. Mom says hello and to tell you she loves you and if you don't come visit soon, she's going to think you forgot all about her."

Sadie was laughing as she rolled her eyes. "Your mom is always being so dramatic. As soon as life calms down, we'll go for a visit."

Melissa's mom, Rachel, had been Sadie's mom's best friend and had lived next door until a few years ago when she fallen for a man who lived in Befana Bay and had moved up to Washington, leaving her house to Melissa.

Sadie unlocked her front door and waved Melissa inside. Instantly, Cosmo, her brindle-colored Lhasa Apso came running toward her, his tail wagging and his tongue hanging out. He launched himself at her, paws out, and bounced off her leg, seemingly unfazed when he toppled over backward and then hopped right back up.

"You goof," Sadie said, reaching down to pick him up. "Did you miss me? I wasn't gone *that* long, was I?"

Cosmo bathed her face in kisses and then started to whine as his body wiggled uncontrollably.

"I know. I know. You need to go out." She put him down and led the way to the back door. As soon as she opened it, he darted out, watered his favorite bush, and then rushed back in. Cosmo wasn't one for hanging around outside by himself.

"Your dog is such a nut," Melissa said, reaching for a treat in the jar right next to the back door.

"That's what I love about him." Sadie filled Cosmo's food dish even as he ran off with his treat. She knew he'd be back in seconds to wolf down his dinner. Then she looked at Melissa. "Are you hungry? I'm making pesto chicken pasta."

"If I wasn't, I am now." Melissa walked into the kitchen and opened the fridge like she owned the place. She pulled out a bottle of pinot grigio. "Wine?"

"Do you even have to ask?" Sadie said with a chuckle.

After Melissa poured the wine, the worked as a team to put dinner together, and when it was finally done, they sat at the table with hot garlic bread, their chicken pesto pasta, and fresh glasses of wine.

"To friends who cook," Melissa said, clinking her glass to Sadie's.

"To friends," Sadie corrected and smiled at her.

"Okay," Melissa said. "Spill. I've been dying here. What's going on with the record deal?"

"Oh man," Sadie said, shaking her head. "You have no idea

what you've missed." Melissa had been gone for two weeks, and Sadie felt like she'd lived a lifetime since she'd last seen her friend.

Her friend looked deadly serious when she asked, "Do we need more wine for this?"

"Yes," Sadie said solemnly even though they both had full glasses.

"I'll keep the bottle on hand," her friend promised. "Now, start with the audition. How did that go?"

Sadie launched into the entire story about how she'd flirted with King before they sang together and then how he'd bolted when he'd realized who she was. She covered the scene at the brewery, when she'd run into him on the trail, and then finally their day of working together in the studio.

Melissa sat back in her chair, looking stunned. "You're saying that King McGrath is *the* Kevin? The guy you met in Westhaven?"

"The very same," Sadie said. Melissa had been the one person that Sadie had told about Kevin and about how heartbroken she'd been when her father forced her to move to Salem.

"That's... crazy," she said, her eyes wide. But then a slow smile claimed her lips. "This is going to be the greatest love story of all time. Met as kids. Bonded over childhood traumas. Ripped apart by circumstance. And then a decade later you reunite and cut a hit record. Add in the enemies-to-lovers trope, and the movie is going to be off the charts. You need to get Cameron and Miranda on it ASAP."

"I think you've had too much wine." Sadie took a bite of garlic bread as she eyed her friend. "Good thing you don't have to drive home later."

"I'm not drunk... yet." Melissa sighed softly. "Look at

you… destined for an epic love story, and here I am, still wondering if I'll ever find Mr. Right. Or even Mr. Right Now."

"Does that mean you broke it off with Linus?" He was the guy she'd been casually seeing for the past couple of months.

"Yep." She gave Sadie a look that said she was one hundred percent over it. "I found out he's dating his stepsister."

Sadie choked on a bite of pasta and coughed until her eyes watered. "I'm sorry," she finally sputtered. "Stepsister?"

"Yeah. I guess their parents were married for a couple of years when they were teenagers, and good old Linus has had the hots for her ever since. He told me, 'You're a nice girl, Melissa, but I have to follow my heart.' More like follow his wanker. Jackass."

"So they aren't stepsiblings anymore?" Sadie asked, knowing that was hardly the point.

"No. But still." She jabbed her fork into her pasta as she shook her head. "I'm the worst at picking men."

"True," Sadie agreed. The one before Linus had wanted Melissa to enter a thrupple with his best girlfriend, Charli. And the one before that had wanted her to quit her job, sell her house, and then fund a backpacking trip around the world while he contributed nothing. "I think you need me to pick the next one."

Melissa raised her hand and said, "I'm in. Nothing can be worse than this last year of losers."

"It's a deal." Sadie winked at her and dug into her pasta.

Her friend however, looked down at her phone and frowned.

"What is it? Is your mom texting or something?" Sadie asked her.

Her friend shook her head and then bent over her screen, making her dark curls hide her face.

"Mel? What's going on?" Sadie asked.

When Melissa lifted her head to look at Sadie, she looked apologetic.

"What—"

"Here." Melissa shoved her phone at Sadie. "Look at the headline."

Sadie's eyes instantly fixated on the picture staring back at her. She frantically scanned the online article for a publication date, and when she saw it was just five minutes ago, she wanted to vomit.

Because right there on the front page of the largest gossip blog in Hollywood was King McGrath kissing some barely-legal girl. She pressed a hand to her stomach, trying to curb the nausea.

"Sadie?" Melissa asked.

"Yeah?" she answered without looking at her friend. She was afraid if she did, she'd start crying, and that was the last thing she was going to do over some fledgling rock star who appeared to have a taste for groupies.

"Want me to kick his ass? Cause I will. I'll grab my car keys right now and— Hell, I'll call a taxi and head over there right this minute and give him the knuckle sandwich he deserves."

"Knuckle sandwich? What are you, eighty?"

She laughed. "That's what my grandpa used to say when he was warning boys away from my mom. Or so he says."

Sadie felt Cosmo move so that he was leaning against her leg. It was something he always did when he wanted to give her comfort. She reached down and pulled him into her arms. "Mama's okay, sweet pea. Just another day where a man is being gross."

"I'm sorry, honey," Melissa said. "That stinks."

Sadie waved her comment away. "There's nothing to be sorry about. It's not like we're anything other than singing partners." She let out a sardonic laugh. "I mean, it was only today that we cleared the air between us. There's no relationship to speak of."

It's not like she had a right to be jealous. Though she could be icked out by the age difference. Sadie handed Melissa her phone. "Let's stop talking about King McGrath and browse that dating app you have. Maybe we can both find someone."

"I'm one hundred percent on board with that," Melissa said, beaming at her. "But first, let's finish dinner and move on to dessert so it won't be so grim when we start looking at the options out there."

Sadie smirked. "That's the spirit." She gave Cosmo a kiss on his head before placing him back down at her feet. Then she pushed the rest of her dinner around while Melissa inhaled her pasta and told her all about the celebrity sightings she'd had while she was in Befana Bay. Apparently they were filming an epic fantasy series that featured a coven with dragon familiars.

"I could really use a dragon familiar," Melissa said with a wistful sigh. "Can you imagine me riding in on one to my next date? That'd be badass."

By the time dinner was over, Melissa had managed to pull Sadie out of her funk that had set in after seeing King splashed all over the tabloids, and she was humming to herself as she dished out a couple pieces of pie.

"What's that song you're singing?" Melissa asked as she

made coffee for them both. They'd finished off the wine, and since they both had to work tomorrow, they'd opted not to open another bottle.

"Huh?" Sadie grabbed the pie plates as she blinked at her friend.

"You're humming something. What is it?"

"Oh." Sadie chuckled to herself. "It's the song King and I are working on. I was just... I dunno, enjoying the melody I guess."

"I really like it. Can you sing it for me?" Melissa asked.

"Seriously? Now, without the music or King here?"

"Yeah, why not? Your voice is gorgeous."

Sadie bit her bottom lip. "Okay, but only if you tell me how awesome I am afterward, 'cause I don't think I can take another blow to my ego tonight."

Melissa laughed and raised her hand. "I swear to the goddess."

"Okay, you asked for it." Sadie cleared her throat and started to sing. Immediately, Melissa's emotions washed over her, making Sadie's skin prickle with both jealousy and awe. Her friend was proud of her but envious of her talent. But then suddenly, Melissa's mood turned wistful and melancholy as Sadie started to sing about lost love and second chances. Regret washed over Sadie, and she couldn't help but wonder who was on Melissa's mind.

When the song was over, Sadie looked over at her friend and caught her wiping away a tear. "Melissa! Why are you crying?"

"It's... beautiful, Sadie. Absolutely beautiful. That's all." Melissa flung her arms around her friend and hugged her tightly. "I am soooo proud of you."

Sadie let out a soft chuckle, hugged her back, and said,

"Thank you. I hope everyone else likes it as much as you do. Otherwise, it's back to the drawing board for me."

"Oh, they will," she insisted. "Trust me."

"I'll try." Sadie really wanted to believe it, but she preferred to keep her expectations in check. If it all went to hell, she didn't want to be caught flat-footed.

They sat in the living room on the couch with their pie and coffee as they browsed the dating site.

"Look, Sadie. This guy says he has a twin," Melissa said. "And he's hot AF."

"Is his twin on there, too?" Sadie asked jokingly.

"Let's see." She did some digging and came up with his profile. "Yep. We should message them. If it works out, we could end up sisters-in-law."

Sadie had mostly been kidding about finding someone to date on the app, but the guy was hot, so… "Message them. Let's see if they're up for a double date."

Melissa cackled. "Oh, this is going to be fun."

CHAPTER 7

"Are you ever going to get off that couch?" Briggs asked King. It had been three days since he'd been assaulted by the fan, and the gossip sites had been on fire, trying to figure out who King's new girlfriend might be.

"Sure. In about an hour when I need to go back into the studio." King took a long sip of his coffee and did his morning check of what had been said about him overnight.

"Austin called you in?" Briggs looked surprised. "I didn't know he wanted to do more recording today."

"I just got a text about ten minutes ago. Apparently he wants to try a few more things, make sure the arrangement is perfect before we debut it at the brewery this Friday."

"Well, thank the gods for that. I was starting to think you were growing roots right there on my couch."

King shot him an irritated glance. "If you'd been mauled by someone and then splashed all over the internet, I bet you wouldn't be in a hurry to show your face around town either."

"There's a different between laying low out of the

spotlight and hibernating indoors without even showering for three days," Briggs said, wrinkling his nose and taking a step back as if to imply that King was more than a little ripe.

King just laughed. "I showered… at least once."

"Uh-huh. If you say so." Briggs walked toward the kitchen. "Go shower while I make breakfast."

"Yes, Mom." Clutching his coffee mug, King retreated to the bathroom. Forty-five minutes later, he emerged feeling human again.

"What the hell were you doing in there?" Briggs asked. He was already at the sink, doing the dirty dishes. "Changing your clothes ten times to make sure you picked just the right outfit?"

"Ha-ha," King said in a flat tone. "Where's that breakfast you promised me?"

"In the oven. You've got about ten minutes." Briggs turned the water off and headed out of the kitchen to finish getting ready for work.

King poured another cup of coffee, retrieved the waffles, and let out a groan when he bit into the nutmeg-flavored goodness. When Briggs walked back in, King said, "Marry me?"

"Do I get access to half your bank account?" Briggs asked.

"Sure."

"Okay, but I'm gonna need this to be an open marriage."

They both laughed.

"What got you so relaxed this morning?" Briggs asked, eyeing him with interest. "It wouldn't have anything to do with seeing a certain singer this morning, would it?"

"Nope," King lied. "I'm not into Sadie. I'm taken, remember?" He pointed at his bare ring finger. "You're going to have to do something about this."

"Hope you like those rings they used to have in candy machines, 'cause that's all I can afford. Now put your plate in the dishwasher. It's time to go."

Smiling to himself, King did as he was told and followed his friend out to the black SUV.

∽

"Good morning," Austin called as King and Briggs walked into the studio.

"Morning." King smiled at Sadie, who was sitting in a chair and eyeing him from across the room.

She quickly glanced away, looking slightly annoyed.

"Morning," Briggs said, taking his seat at the control board.

Sadie glanced at him. "Hello, Briggs."

Briggs nodded at her and winked. "Ready to do this thing?"

"As ready as I can be, I guess," she said.

King stood next to her, placing a hand on her shoulder. "You'll be great. You always are."

She glanced at his hand and shrugged slightly, clearly indicating she didn't want him to touch her.

King pulled his hand away, wondering what in the world had happened since the last time he'd talked to Sadie. He hadn't expected her to be so cool toward him. "What's going on?"

The question had been to Sadie, but Austin was the one who answered. "I just want to try a couple of key changes and add some background vocals for the production. Ready to get started?"

"Sure. Do you want both of us in the booth?" King asked,

hoping whatever was going on with Sadie that she'd be able to let it go when they started working.

"Yes, please."

King held the door open for Sadie and watched as she moved stiffly into the room. Something was definitely up with her.

They each sat on the stools and turned their attention to Austin.

"Give me just a minute to get set up," Austin said as Briggs made some adjustments to the board.

"Did you have a good weekend?" King asked Sadie.

She sucked in a breath. "I mostly just worked."

"I bet it was busy with Halloween coming up," he tried again.

"Yeah."

He nodded, and then silence fell between them.

Awkward.

"So," he said, trying to fill the dead space. "I seem to remember back when we were younger, that you had a notebook of lyrics you used to work on. Are you still trying your hand at songwriting?"

"Not really," she said with a tiny shrug.

"Are you interested in trying again?" He wasn't sure where he was going with this, but the words just kept coming. "Because if you are, I was thinking that maybe we could—"

"No," she said, cutting him off. "I don't think that's a good idea."

He was about to ask why not when Austin said, "Okay, I think we're ready. Sadie, we'll start with you, all right?"

"Sure," she said, putting her headphones on. "Just tell me what you want."

For the next half hour, King was captivated by everything about her. The emotion on her face when she sang certain lyrics, her tiny movements as she hit certain notes, and most of all, the way her voice just seemed to wind right through his very being. It wasn't an exaggeration to say he was certain she'd cast a spell over him.

"Excellent," Austin said. "Okay, now I'd like to work on the chorus again. King? Are you ready? I want both of your voices together."

He cleared his throat and adjusted his headphones. "Sure."

The music started, and King turned to Sadie. Their eyes met, and once again, he was completely lost in the magic that bound them together while they were singing. For once in his life, he didn't feel like he was carrying the weight of the world on his shoulders, and he wanted to live in the moment forever.

The session was like that all day, and then just before five, Austin said, "That was perfect! Just perfect."

Sadie beamed at King, but then it was almost as if a dark cloud settled over her as she wiped the smile from her face and glanced away.

"I think we can call it a day," Austin said. "We'll get this mixed and send it over in a few days."

"Sounds good." Sadie practically leaped from her stool and bolted out of the booth.

King just watched her go as the magic that had filled him quickly vanished, leaving him feeling empty and frustrated.

"Hold on," Austin said before she ran out of the studio. "We have business to discuss."

King joined them in the control booth and sat in a chair next to Briggs.

"I want you two to debut this song at the festival on

Halloween night. We're going to drop the single that day, and we'll have media set up and go live on socials. You'll also need to do King's other song to fill the set, so it'll be up to you two to practice and make sure you have this down cold before that. Understand?"

Halloween was just a week away. It meant they likely were going to have to get together each day to make sure they were ready to be blasted all over the internet.

King nodded. "Yeah, okay."

"Uh, sure," Sadie said with a tentative nod. "As long as we can schedule it around my work schedule."

"Are you working Halloween night?" Austin asked.

"I think so, but I can work it out." She bit down on her bottom lip, looking more skeptical than she sounded. "I'll switch or something. Though if I have to practice, I'm just not sure how that will work. Don't worry. I'll figure it out."

"You know, Sadie, this is why we give you an advance. So you're free to promote and record when we need you to," Austin said. "Maybe it's time to think about reducing your hours at the brewery."

"Right," she said and then let out a nervous laugh. "That's weird to think about, I guess."

"Get used to it because this song is going to be a major hit. And then you and King are going to be all over the country playing it for your fans."

King could only hope. The thought of being out on the road with Sadie was a literal dream come true. At least it would be if he could figure out why she was giving him the cold shoulder.

Sadie nodded and then turned to King. "I'll text you my schedule so we can work something out." Then she took off out the door.

"Hey," Briggs said, turning to him. "I'm starving. Which is it tonight? Pizza or the brewery?"

"Pizza," King said. "Give me a minute, though." He exited the door to the back parking lot and scanned the area. There, just a few cars down, he spotted Sadie opening the door of her Camry. "Sadie, wait."

She jumped and pressed a hand to her chest as she turned to look at him. "Oh gosh, you startled me. Does Austin want us back in there?"

"No," he said, running his hand through his dark curls. "I just came to find out what's wrong. You sang great today, but you can't fool me. Something's off. Is it anything I can help with?"

"Nothing's wrong," she said, crossing her arms over her chest.

He raised both eyebrows. "Are you sure about that? If nothing's wrong, then why are you having trouble even looking at me today. Did I do something to upset you?"

"No." She pressed her lips together into a thin line. "Not at all. I just… You know what? Never mind. I wouldn't want to keep you from your groupies. I'm sure they're waiting for you somewhere." She reached for her door handle and opened the door.

"Groupies?" he choked out incredulously. "You think I'm hanging out with groupies? Where did that come from?"

She spun back around. "I saw the picture of you kissing that girl, King. It's all over the internet. And I know we're not a thing or anything, and it's none of my business what you do, but she looked like she was barely fourteen, and I just—"

"Whoa!" He held his hands up, trying to process everything she'd just said. She knew they weren't a thing? Did that imply she might be interested? It kind of sounded like it. But then maybe not since she thought he was the kind of guy who'd not only make out with random fans, in public no less, but that he'd do that with underage kids. "First of all, I had nothing to do with that kiss. That girl all but assaulted me as her friends videoed the entire thing. And second, she wasn't fourteen. I didn't see her ID or anything, but I'm pretty sure they were all legal drinking age. If not, they were close. Not that I should have to be explaining any of this."

"No, you don't have to explain anything to me," she agreed. "I shouldn't have brought it up. Can we just forget this conversation?"

"I will if you will," he said, feeling more violated than ever. He hated being pawed at by strangers, but he hated it even more when people he knew thought that he somehow welcomed the entire thing.

She nodded. "I better go. Melissa and I are meeting some people at the harvest festival."

It was then that her thoughts came through loud and clear.

I never should have said yes to this date. If it wasn't so late, I'd just cancel and curl up on the couch with Cosmo and never show my face again. Holy hell, King must think I'm an idiot.

He wanted to respond, tell her he didn't think anything of the sort, but he didn't want to embarrass her or have her think he was intentionally reading her thoughts.

"Yeah. You don't want to be late," he said, trying to be gracious. "Text me your schedule, and we'll figure out when we can get together to rehearse."

"I will," she promised. Then she glanced up at him one more time. "I'm sorry, King. Whatever happened with you and that fan, I never should have brought it up."

He blew out a breath. "If this song is as successful as we

think it's going to be, you'll learn soon enough that people will manipulate your photos, videos, words, or anything that will fit their narrative. Trust me on this."

She nodded once, climbed in her car, and then backed up and headed out of the parking lot.

Frustrated, King walked back into the studio where Briggs was waiting for him.

"Where's Austin?" King asked.

"He left. Said he was meeting his girl, Brinn, at the festival."

King nodded and then said, "Let's skip the pizza and go to the harvest festival. I'm suddenly having a craving for festival food."

"Seriously?" Briggs asked, perking up. "I thought for sure you'd want to lay low after that fan fiasco earlier this week, but if you're up for it, I'm game."

"Let's go."

CHAPTER 8

Sadie followed Melissa through the festival, enjoying the scents of caramel apples, pumpkin tarts, buttery popcorn, and her favorite festival food ever—funnel cakes. "Wait," Sadie said as she veered toward the cart with the funnel cakes. "I need one of these immediately."

"Now?" Melissa sounded horrified. "You don't really want to meet your date with powdered sugar all over your face, do you?"

"You have very little faith in my ability to eat without turning into a toddler." Sadie stepped up to the window and glanced back. "Do you want one?"

"Oh, no. I'm not going to have sticky fingers when I meet the man I'm going to marry."

Sadie rolled her eyes and turned back to the teenager working the booth. "One funnel cake and a bottle of water. Thanks." She paid, and a moment later she had her order in hand. "Isn't this roughly where we're supposed to meet our dates?"

"Yeah. There's the Ferris wheel." She pointed to the lit-up ride behind them.

Sadie scanned the area, spotted a group of wooden picnic tables, and said, "Let's sit there while I wolf this down."

"They're gonna show up while you're shoving fried dough in your face," Melissa admonished.

"No they aren't. They said seven. It's only six-twenty. There's plenty of time to tackle this and clean up after." Sadie took a seat and dug into her funnel cake.

"You look like a rabid raccoon," Melissa said with a light chuckle.

"I feel like one too," Sadie said around a bite of the yummy goodness. "You just don't know what you're missing."

Melissa eyed the funnel cake, staring longingly at the fried dough.

"You know you want some." Sadie stabbed a piece of the cake and held the plastic fork up to her friend. "Go on. It's probably the best thing you'll put in your mouth all night."

"Goddess, I hope that's not true. If this date works out, I was planning on taking that gorgeous man home with me." She grabbed the fork and did her own impression of a rabid raccoon. "Oh my effing hell. This is delicious."

"I told you." Sadie took the fork back from her friend. "You know it's not too late to get your own funnel cake."

Melissa stared longingly at the funnel cake booth but ultimately shook her head. When she turned her attention back to Sadie, she pointed at her face. "You have powdered sugar on your chin."

Sadie took one of her napkins and wet it from her bottle of water and cleaned up her chin. "Better?"

"For now."

Sadie knew her friend was regretting turning down the funnel cake when she wouldn't stop staring at the plate in front of her. "Here." Sadie pushed it toward her. "Take it."

"Are you sure?" Melissa asked, even as she dug in for a bite.

Sadie laughed and jumped up to go get herself another one from the booth. After she had her new funnel cake in her hands, she started to walk back to the table but stopped dead in her tracks when she spotted King and Briggs standing in front of a booth that advertised fried pumpkin pie on a stick. The worker handed one to each of them and what looked to be a can of whipped cream to Briggs.

Should she just walk back over to her table and pretend she didn't see them? Immediately, she wondered if she still had powdered sugar on her face. Melissa had been right when she'd said that stuff got everywhere no matter how careful you tried to be.

She decided she didn't want to look like a fool in front of King and quickly headed back to her table.

"King is here," Melissa said as soon as Sadie sat down.

"I know." Sadie didn't look back while she cut the funnel cake in half and deposited a portion onto Melissa's plate.

"That's too much," her friend said even as she took another bite.

"Eat what you want, leave the rest," Sadie said, wondering if she could choke down whatever her friend didn't eat.

Before she could find out, Sadie heard someone call out, "There he is! It's King McGrath!"

The announcement was followed by high-pitched squealing as a group of six or seven college-age girls dressed as scantily clad sexy witches ran toward King and Briggs.

King froze like a deer in the headlights while Briggs

automatically stepped in front of him, trying to shield him from the onslaught. But it didn't work. They swarmed in from the side and behind. And then one of them had the audacity to walk up right behind King and wrap her arms around him as she rested her chin on his shoulder.

Immediately, King gently pried her hands off him and stepped away, putting as much space between them as he could without knocking down other festival goers. He looked highly uncomfortable with his shoulders hunched and his hands in his pockets as he said something to them she couldn't hear.

One of the girls sauntered up to him holding out a wand. She gave him a sexy little smile as she pressed the tip of the wand to his chest and then slowly lowered it until it reached the top of his jeans.

King reached down and grabbed it, stopping her from doing something obscene.

If it had been Sadie, she'd have broken the wand in half and then would've needed to be restrained so she didn't stab someone with it.

Briggs was talking and moving forward, trying to get the women to back off.

The one with the wand appeared to be pouting as she clung to King's arm.

His expression was blank as he stiffly tried to disentangle himself, and Sadie got the distinct impression that he was only seconds from losing his shit. When she spotted two of the women filming the interaction, she recalled what he'd told her about how people would manipulate anything to create a narrative. It was likely why he was tolerating their invasion, and it made her sick to her stomach.

Her funnel cake forgotten, Sadie jumped up and strode over to King's side.

"Sadie—" he started, weariness in his gorgeous blue eyes.

She walked up next to him, nudged the overly aggressive witch out of the way, and wrapped her arm around his waist. Smiling up at him, she said, "Hey. There you are. I wondered where you'd got off to."

"Uh, Briggs and I got a little hungry." He held up his pumpkin pie on a stick.

"That's good news, because I have half a funnel cake over there, and I need you to finish it off." She nodded toward the table where Melissa was staring at them, her mouth open. Sadie glanced at the barely dressed witches. "Thanks for entertaining my boyfriend for me. I've got it from here."

Sadie slipped her arm through his and guided him over to her table. She pointed at the funnel cake. "See, I really did have some fried dough for you to eat."

King laughed as he sat at the table and then tugged her to sit next to him. As soon as she was seated, he wrapped an arm around her shoulders and kissed her on the temple, making a shiver go down her spine. "Thank you for the save, Lewis. I owe you one."

"No you don't," she said, trying to appear normal and certain she was failing. All she wanted to do was lean into King, revel in his familiar warmth, and spend the rest of the evening just like this. But Melissa would kill her if she bailed on the double date.

Sadie shifted to put a tiny bit of distance between her and King just for her own preservation. Then she eyed the sexy witches as they reluctantly moved on. "You don't owe me anything. Consider it even after I misjudged you. Seeing how uncomfortable you were with that scene, I just can't picture you hooking up with random fans."

"He definitely doesn't do that," Briggs said, eyeing Sadie's funnel cake. "Are you going to eat that?"

"Here." Sadie pushed it toward him as he generously sprayed his pumpkin pie on a stick with the whipped cream. Then he sprayed it all over the funnel cake, and Sadie gasped. "What did you just do?"

Briggs was too busy chewing a giant bite of deep-fried pie to answer.

King shook his head. "Briggs kinda has a thing for whipped cream."

"Kinda?" Melissa asked. "Looks to me like he has a full-on love affair with it."

Briggs's shoulders shook as he laughed silently.

"I think you didn't feed him soon enough," Sadie observed. "Look at him. If one of us reaches for the funnel cake, we might lose a hand."

Briggs nodded happily as he shoved a generous bite of the funnel cake into his mouth.

"I like a man who knows his way around food," Melissa said, pumping her eyebrows at him.

He let his gaze travel over her as if he were assessing her for the first time. When he swallowed, he gave her a sexy little half grin and said, "I know my way around a lot of things."

Melissa giggled. Actually giggled. Sadie didn't think she'd heard that sound from her friend since they were fourteen. Her bestie handed Briggs a napkin as she said, "I just bet you do."

"Melissa?" A tall, dark-haired guy with a swimmer's body asked.

His clone chimed in with, "Sadie?"

"Jasper, Kasper!" Melissa cried as she jumped up off her bench. "You're here." She hugged each of them quickly and then glanced at Sadie, who had yet to get up off the bench. "Uh, Sadie? Are you ready to go?"

Sadie absolutely wasn't ready to go, but she couldn't stand up her date just because she was crushing hard on King McGrath. Reluctantly, she stood. "Yes, of course." She glanced down at King and felt a flash of raw jealousy as he stared at the twins, his jaw tight. Sadie put her hand on King's shoulder. "You okay?"

"Sure," he said, not taking his eyes from their dates.

She stifled a sigh. "Okay. Have a good night. I'll text you tomorrow."

"Sure. Enjoy yourselves." There was resignation in his expression as he nodded, and Sadie marveled that she could no longer feel his emotions. He'd put a lock on them, and from what she knew of the general public, most people had no idea how to do that. But King wasn't just anyone. He was King McGrath, a minor celebrity who'd had to learn how to navigate the world when everything eventually ended up online. She was certain that wasn't a coincidence.

Feeling as if she had lead in her feet, Sadie was introduced to Jasper and Kasper, who turned out to be two of the most boring men she'd ever met.

Melissa and Jasper walked in front of Sadie and Kasper as Kasper spent an entire hour talking about a new steam mop he'd bought for the house he and his brother shared. And when he moved on to robot vacuum cleaners, Sadie was ready to stab herself in the eye just to have a reason to escape.

Just when she thought Kasper was ready to take a breath,

he pointed at Ms. Celeste's tarot table and said, "Look! It's Celeste. We should get readings."

"We should?" Sadie asked, already knowing there was zero chance of her opening up to a tarot reader.

"Absolutely! If we do it this year, when we come back next year, we can evaluate how accurate the readers were. Fun, huh?" Kasper was so earnest and sweet, and he looked like a Greek god. On paper, he seemed like a perfect match. But in person, there wasn't even a hint of a spark. She wasn't gonna make it the entire date, much less a whole year.

"Tell you what, you go, and then I'll decide if it was worth it," she said, giving him a tiny nudge toward the tarot reader.

He sat down and asked, "What do I need to do? I'm a first timer, so…"

She reassured him he had nothing to worry about and then gave the blandest reading on the planet. It turned out that according to the reader, Kasper was due for some professional success. But personal relationships? There was no girlfriend for him in the cards at this time.

"No girlfriend?" He looked at Sadie. "Are you sure?"

"Yes. In fact, there's one you like, but she's going to go her own way. Sooner rather than later," Ms. Celeste confirmed.

"That's my cue," Sadie said brightly. She walked over to Kasper, shook his hand, and said, "Thanks for a nice evening, but I've got to work tomorrow, so it's best if I head out."

"So soon?" Kasper asked. "But we haven't even gotten to see what they're playing at the open theater tonight. If it's *Carrie*, you're going to hate yourself for leaving."

"It's a chance I'm willing to take," she said and waved as she strode off, back to her little house on the edge of the woods with the best dog in the world. Back to her sanctuary where she'd be free to dream of King and forget that disastrous date had ever happened.

CHAPTER 9

*K*ing knocked on the front door of Sadie's one-story, sea-green cottage and smiled to himself. There were fake spiderwebs, gargoyles, and a stone black cat decorating the porch. But the lawn was the truly spectacular show. She had put out headstones and added plastic skeleton hands to make it look like zombies were rising from the graves. There was also a skeleton cat chasing a skeleton dog and a statue of a haggard witch overseeing the scene.

It was exactly the way he'd imagined it would be for Halloween. Back in Westhaven when they were just kids, Sadie had often talked of the house she'd grown up in. How she and her mother had gone overboard decorating for the holidays. It was one of the only times she'd spoken about her mom without tearing up.

He glanced at the porch swing and had a sudden vision of them sitting right there, cuddled together as they watched the snow trickle down in the dead of winter. His heart fluttered as joy filled all his empty spaces.

Anxious to see Sadie, he knocked and then quickly rang the doorbell.

Frantic barking came from inside and was quickly followed by the door being tugged open and Sadie saying, "Hush, Cosmo. It's okay. King is here to work on that song."

The brindle-colored dog ignored her order and continued to bark and growl at King.

"Do I need to worry about losing a limb?" King asked, only half joking.

"No." Sadie rolled her eyes and picked up the small but sturdy dog. "He'll calm down in a few minutes. Come on in."

King followed her into the house and took in the comfortable, eclectic style. The floors were a rustic hardwood, and she'd furnished the living room with an overstuffed couch and chair. The walls were filled with colorful paintings and prints that were a mix of depictions of Keating Hollow and family photos. "Your house is great."

"Thanks," she said. "It's not much, but it's mine."

He shook his head. "This is your family home, and it shows. I'm glad I finally got to see it."

Her face flushed pink as she hugged her dog to her chest. He'd stopped growling, but he was still eyeing King with suspicion. "Let me just get Cosmo a chew stick so it keeps him occupied while we get started. Have a seat and I'll be right back."

King nodded, but instead of sitting, he went to the wood fireplace mantle and studied the photos there. There were a handful of Sadie and her friend Melissa. But mostly they were photos of Sadie and her mom. He picked up one that was a birthday celebration. Sadie looked exactly how he'd remembered her as a teenager, although there was a light in her eyes and an ease she hadn't carried with her when he'd known her back then. It made his heart break for the teenager in the photo.

"I brought water," Sadie said as she walked back into the room with Cosmo at her side, a chewy stick in his mouth. The dog ran to his pet bed and gave his full attention to his treat. When Sadie spotted King holding one of her photos, she stopped in her tracks. "That was my sixteenth birthday," she said quietly.

"It looks like it was a good one," he said as he carefully placed the photo back where he'd found it. "I don't have any family photos like this."

Her expression turned to pity. "King, that's—"

"It's shit," he got out before she could finish her sentence. Shrugging, he added, "It's okay. I have long accepted that I just didn't do well in the parental lottery. I'm glad you did better."

She placed the waters on her coffee table and came over to him. Without saying a word, she wrapped her arms around him, giving him a hug.

King's arms went around her, and he placed his cheek on the top of her head, soaking in the love she'd always given so freely. He'd have been happy to stay there forever, but he feared if he didn't put distance between them, he'd never let her go. As he pulled back, he said, "I'm okay. Promise."

"I know you are." She gave him a soft smile. "That doesn't mean you don't need a hug every now and then from someone who cares about you."

He raised his eyebrows. "You're saying you care about me?"

Sadie glanced away briefly but then met his gaze again and said, "Of course I do. I always have. I hope you know that."

Had he? If she'd asked him that a few weeks ago, he'd have said no. Not after the way she'd disappeared from his life when they were younger. But now? After hearing how her father had forced her to move to a town she'd never been to before and ripped her away from her grandmother so shortly after her mother had passed, he could completely understand how a confused and upset teenager wouldn't handle that situation very well.

When he didn't answer, she cleared her throat. "Anyway, we should get to work. My home studio is this way."

"You have a home studio?" King asked, surprised. When she'd invited him over to rehearse, he'd figured they'd just be singing in her living room. It wasn't ideal, but since Austin had another artist recording in the studio that week, it was better than nothing.

"Yeah. I turned my mom's office into one so I could… I don't know, mess around, I guess. It's where I did my demo for Austin." She grabbed the waters and led him into a small bedroom just off the living room. There was a guitar on a stand in the corner, a keyboard against the wall, and a computer set up on a desk with a mic on a desk-mounted mic stand. "It's not much, but—"

"This is perfect," King said as he glanced around. "Do you have another mic and stand?"

She shook her head. "I've never needed another one."

"That's fine. We can share." He pulled up one of the chairs and took a seat. "Do you mind if we record it so we can hear how we sound?"

"Not at all." Sadie took her place in the seat next to him and fiddled with her equipment for a few minutes before she said, "Okay. Just let me know when you're ready and I'll start the music track."

"Ready," he said.

They spent the next few hours recording their rehearsals and playing them back until they were both satisfied with their performances.

Finally King sat back in his chair and said, "I don't know about you, but I'm ready for dinner."

Sadie glanced at her phone. "Whew, no wonder my stomach is trying to eat itself. It's after seven already." Then she bit down on her bottom lip. "Did you want to stay? I can see if I can rummage something up. Or if you have plans or are just ready to take off, I get that, too. I'm sure you weren't expecting to stay late or anything."

King couldn't help the smile that claimed his lips. She was rambling. It was something she'd done when they were teenagers when she was nervous, but he hadn't experienced it since he'd walked back into her life a couple of weeks ago. "I don't have plans. I'd love to stay for dinner."

"Oh, okay. Well, let's see what we can find. I suppose if all else fails, we can order pizza," she said as she walked out of the room.

Pizza again? King swallowed a groan. He and Briggs had eaten their weight in pizza since King had arrived. There were only so many options for takeout in Keating Hollow, and neither had made it a priority to stock the fridge, so they'd been eating out far too often.

As King followed Sadie through the living room, her dog popped up out of his bed and shot toward him, his teeth bared.

"Cosmo!" Sadie cried. "No. Sit!"

The dog came to a sudden stop and promptly dropped his rear to the floor, but he was still vibrating with the urge to continue his attack.

"I'm so sorry, King. He's a little protective, but it's not usually this bad," Sadie said.

"He probably just needs to get used to me." King took a step forward and then kneeled down so that he was on the dog's level. "Hey, boy."

Cosmo snarled.

King chuckled softly. "You're a good boy, aren't you? Protecting your mama. She's lucky you're here." He curled his hand into a fist and offered it to the dog, letting Cosmo get used to his scent. "I'm not gonna hurt your mama."

Cosmo eyed him suspiciously but had stopped snarling.

"That's good, Cosmo. I'm willing to be friends if you are."

The dogged sniffed King and then looked at Sadie.

"He's okay, Cos," Sadie said. "I promise. You don't need to eat his face."

King stayed perfectly still for what seemed like forever until the fierce little dog's stature suddenly relaxed. He opened his mouth, his tongue hanging out as he panted softly and walked right up to King, placing his head under King's hand.

"What a sweet boy," King said as he scratched the dog's head and then his ears. Cosmo had a look of pure bliss before he flopped down on the floor and rolled onto his back, putting all four paws in the air. King glanced up at Sadie. "Is this normal?"

She laughed. "He wants you to rub his belly. Do that and you'll be his bestie for life."

"Well then, I guess I better give this boy the belly rubs he deserves." King spent the next ten minutes loving on Cosmo and finally, when the dog cuddled up next to him, his head on King's leg, King glanced up, looking for Sadie, but she was nowhere to be found. "Sadie?"

"I'm in the kitchen," she called back.

"That's my cue, buddy," King said to the dog and got to his feet.

Cosmo jumped up, too, and together they went to find Sadie.

"I see my belly rub whore of a dog has thrown me over for another," she said, smiling at them.

"I'm sure the moment you feed him dinner he'll forget all about me." King winked and moved to the sink to wash his hands.

"Ha, that's true."

"So, what did you find in that fridge of yours?" he asked while he dried his hands.

"I hope you don't have a dairy allergy," she said with a smirk. "Cause all I've got is macaroni and cheese."

King looked around for the blue and yellow box but was surprised to see she had a box of pasta shells and real cheese on the counter. "You're going to make homemade mac and cheese?"

"Yeah. If we want to get fancy, we can add bacon and caramelized onions," she said.

"Cheese and bacon?" King lowered himself to one knee, tugged a ring off his right hand, and held it out to her. "Sadie Lewis, will you marry me?"

"Get up," Sadie said with a laugh as she shook her head. "At least wait until you taste it before you make that sort of gesture. You could be signing yourself up for a lifetime of limp bacon and crunchy, undercooked pasta."

"Okay, if you insist." Weirdly disappointed at her immediate dismissal, King climbed to his feet and tried his best to ignore the feeling. "Put me to work."

It didn't take long to put all the ingredients together, and once the dish was in the oven, Sadie opened the fridge and asked, "Beer? Wine? Soda?"

"Beer, please." He walked over to the treat jar on the counter. "Can Cosmo have one of these?"

The dog immediately started jumping on his leg.

"Yeah, but for future reference, he knows that jar. And if you go anywhere near it, he'll pester you until he gets what he wants."

"You wouldn't do that, would you, buddy?" King asked as he reached into the jar for the treat. Cosmo sat, his eyes tracking the treat in King's fingers. "See, you're a good boy." He gave the dog the treat and nearly lost a finger because the pup was so excited to take it.

"Oops, I should have warned you. Nothing gets between him and his food," Sadie said, handing him a bottle from the Keating Hollow Brewery.

"I'll remember that."

King had just sat on the couch when his phone started to ring. He glanced at it and saw that it was his mother again. He immediately declined it. The phone started ringing almost instantly, and King swore under his breath as he put his phone on silent. She'd been calling ever since he'd transferred money to her account, and King had no doubt she was unhappy with the amount.

"Everything okay?" Sadie asked as she took a seat next to him.

"Yeah, sure," he said automatically, but then he wondered why he was lying to her. She and Briggs were the only two people who knew anything about his history with his parents. "Actually, that was my mother."

Sadie turned to give him her full attention. "Your biological mother?"

SONG OF THE WITCH

King snorted derisively. "Definitely my bio mom. Briggs and I don't talk to our foster parents."

"You don't? I thought you liked them," she said. "What happened?"

"I guess this is where I confess that I wasn't completely honest about my homelife," he said, staring at his beer. "It wasn't the sanctuary I led you to believe."

Sadie reached over and placed a comforting hand on his thigh but didn't say anything.

He glanced at her, grateful there wasn't any pity in her eyes. "I lied because I didn't want you to see me as a tragic castoff. Being discarded by my own parents and being homeless wasn't something I'd wish on anyone. I guess I just wanted to be seen as wanted, so I told you that my foster parents were loving people who'd opened their home and their hearts. But in reality, they just wanted the extra money from the government. The moment the money stopped, they told me and Briggs we were on our own."

"That's really messed up." Sadie's eyes flashed with something that looked a lot like hatred. "I'm sorry, King. Neither you nor Briggs deserved that. No child does. I don't care if the government puts an arbitrary age on adulthood. Young adults still need support."

"Yeah," he said, suddenly feeling like something had shifted between them. The energy between them was almost like they were back in Westhaven, where he felt he could share a piece of himself that he kept locked away from the rest of the world. "But it turns out that maybe it was for the best. Briggs and I had each other for support, and at least I gained a brother out of the deal."

"I'm glad you have him." She stared at him for a long

moment before suddenly glancing away and giving her full attention to Cosmo, who was lying at her feet.

"What is it, Sadie?" he asked gently.

She shrugged and then let out a long breath before she looked at him again. "I wish I'd done things differently back then. I could've at least let you know where I was going. Could have called you back after all the messages you left me right after my dad made me leave Westhaven. After we'd been in Salem for about a month, I finally called your house and left a message, but when you didn't call me back, I figured you just didn't want to talk to me. And I didn't blame you at all. So I figured I messed it all up and left you alone after that."

"You called my house?" King asked, his chest suddenly tight.

"Yeah. I left a message on the voice mail."

Anger seethed throughout his body, though he supposed he shouldn't be surprised that whoever had heard the message hadn't bothered to tell him. His foster parents just hadn't cared enough to realize how important that call would have been to him. "Nobody told me that, Sadie. I would have returned that call. If nothing else, I would have wanted to just make sure you were okay."

Tears shone in her eyes as she said, "I really am sorry."

He clasped his hand over hers and squeezed. "So am I."

She squeezed back and said, "We really were just two lost souls back then, weren't we?"

A haunting melody started to play in his mind as a lyric formed. *Just two lost souls, destined to fade into tattered memories, I swore I'd never forget you. Now I'm staring in your eyes, wondering if I'll survive another loss of you.*

King suddenly stood. "We need to go back to the studio."

CHAPTER 10

Sadie stood behind King, her entire body vibrating with emotion. The heart wrenching song that was pouring out of him was tearing her to pieces. It told their story. Of two broken kids meeting when their lives were in turmoil and they needed each other the most, and the suffering they both endured when they were ripped apart. It was love and loss and solace and pain.

And it was the most beautiful thing she'd ever heard.

Without a word, she picked up her guitar and started to strum cords that matched his energy. He looked over at her and nodded his approval.

Sadie felt as if she were transfixed. As if the music was almost making itself and she was nothing but a vessel. Though since King's emotional energy was pouring into her, she supposed that maybe she was. This song, the words, the chords, the vibe, they were one hundred percent coming from King.

And when his voice faded and the last note died out, she

wobbled slightly, feeling as if all of her energy had been drained. She slowly sank onto her chair while they both stared at each other, neither of them saying a word.

It wasn't until Cosmo appeared in the room and pressed into her leg that she finally broke their connection and reached down to pick up her dog. Cosmo snuggled into her and gave her a kiss on her cheek.

"Lucky dog," King said with a small smile.

Sadie opened her mouth to say something, but the timer on her oven went off and she stood so fast she nearly dumped Cosmo on the ground. "Whoops. Sorry, boy." She gently placed him on the floor and then headed into the kitchen, grateful to have a little bit of space. That impromptu recording session had been intense, and she wasn't at all sure what it meant.

As she was taking the mac and cheese out of the oven, King arrived and started rummaging through her cabinets for plates and then her drawers for utensils.

"Thanks," she said, grabbing a couple more beers. If she was going to make it through the night, she was definitely going to need another drink or two. "We just need to let this sit for a few minutes."

King nodded, and while he was setting the table, she got Cosmo his dinner and a fresh bowl of water. Once she was done, she leaned against the counter with her hands in her pockets, not sure what to say.

Thankfully her phone rang, giving her something else to focus on. "Melissa? Hey."

"You've got to do me a huge favor," her friend said.

"Sure. Anything." Sadie went to her drawer to find a serving spoon for the mac and cheese.

"I need you to go out with Kasper again. Jasper says he really likes you and—"

"What?" Sadie was already shaking her head. "That can't be true. I basically walked out on that date. Kasper can't possibly want to see me again."

"Oh, he does. He says that the tarot reading spooked you, and he wants another chance to prove the reading wrong."

Sadie laughed. "He thinks the tarot reading was the problem? Are you serious? The tarot reading was the only decent thing that happened. It gave me an excuse to get out of there. I'm sorry, Mel, but that would just be wasting everyone's time. I'm not interested."

"I know, but Jasper has four tickets to see the Crimson Vamps tomorrow night. Actually, he and Kasper have four tickets, and Jasper is saying that Kasper is freaking out about being a third wheel and threatening not to go unless he has a date. Now Jasper is saying he doesn't want to go if his brother doesn't go, and you know how much I love the Crimson Vamps. Please? Do it for me? I'll owe you big time. I'll... I don't know, mow your lawn, or wash your windows, or cook you dinner for a month."

"Good goddess, don't threaten to cook for me. I might not survive it," Sadie said.

"I'll get takeout then. Please, Sadie? Just one more date? I promise I won't ask again," she pleaded.

There was nothing Sadie wanted to do less than hang out with the boring twins. What did her friend see in Jasper anyway? Likely she was a lot more interested in the band, but one never knew. Her friend didn't have the best picker when it came to men. But Sadie had to admit that Jasper at least seemed harmless. It wouldn't hurt for her to date him for a while. But it would hurt Sadie since she knew she couldn't say no to her friend. "Fine. I'll do it, but you don't owe me anything. You're already letting me and Cosmo stay at your house while it's getting fumigated and the repairs are being done over the next couple weeks. We'll call it even, okay?"

Since Sadie's house needed to be tented for termites and then needed work to repair the damage they'd caused, she and Cosmo needed to vacate for a couple of weeks. Melissa had offered her spare room, and Sadie was more than grateful.

"I'll still do something as a thank you," she said. "My house is your house. You know that. And I know you don't want to do this, but I love you for it. How about I treat us to a day at the spa sometime soon?"

"You don't have to do that."

"Yes, I do," Melissa said. "They're meeting us at the brewery after your shift. I'll see you there." The call ended, and Sadie dropped her phone before burying her face in her hands as she let out a groan.

"Sounds like you have a hot date," King said, his voice tight.

Sadie looked up at him. He had a smile pasted on his face, but it couldn't have been more forced. "Hot is a vast overstatement. If that had been any other person in the world besides Melissa, I would not be in this mess."

"So you really aren't interested?" he asked, sounding unsure.

Sadie let out a bark of laughter as she grabbed the serving spoon. "What about that phone conversation made you think I actually want to go?"

It was his turn to chuckle. "Nothing really. But I had to make sure."

"Why?"

"This is why." He took the spoon from her hand and placed it on the counter. Then he wrapped one arm around her waist and raised his other arm to bury his fingers in her hair. Pulling her impossibly close, he whispered, "I've been wanting to do this since that first night I saw you at the brewery."

Sadie stared at his lips, all thoughts of Jasper and Kasper gone. Gooseflesh popped out on her arms as anticipation sent a tingle up her spine. When he didn't move, she let out a breath and whispered, "Kiss me, King."

His lips turned up into a slow, self-satisfied smile when he said, "My pleasure." He moved in, gently pressing his warm lips to hers.

Suddenly, King's emotions washed over her in a mix of elation and longing. And then impatience as his tongue darted out and he licked at the seam of her lips. Sadie opened for him and just like that, she was lost in the passion. Her hands clutched at his shoulders as her body leaned into his heat. She wanted him. All of him.

All too soon, he ended the kiss and pulled back slightly, pressing his forehead to hers. She stayed perfectly still, breathing him in. She'd never responded to another man the way she responded to King. Every molecule of her being had been in on that kiss, and if he'd taken her to her room, she'd have gone, no questions asked.

The thought startled her, and suddenly she stepped back, not sure where that had come from. She wasn't one to rush into such things, especially when she had no idea where their relationship stood. As of now, they were collaborators and friends. Friends who had to work together for who knew how long with much of that time spent on the road.

"Do you think the mac and cheese is ready now?" King said, his eyes glinting with amusement.

"Huh?" Sadie blinked at him. Then she shook her head. "Yes. Of course." She glanced down at the counter, finding the spoon in the pasta dish, and she got to work portioning out their dinner.

"Hey, Sadie?" King said softly.

"Yeah?"

"You should know that after dinner, I'm planning for a proper make-out session." He winked at her and then grabbed both plates to take them to the table.

Sadie stood in the kitchen, holding onto the counter to give her weak knees a moment to recover. Finally, she took a deep breath and joined him at the table.

The scent of the mac and cheese was so delectable that she started to salivate. Her stomach grumbled with hunger. She placed a hand on her stomach as her cheeks flushed with heat. "Sorry."

"No need to apologize. I'm starving, too." He picked up his fork and grabbed a bite, and the moment the cheesy goodness hit his tongue, his eyes rolled to the back of his head as he let out an obscene moan of pleasure. "Holy balls, Sadie," he said after he swallowed. "This is delicious."

"Thank you." She shoved a forkful in her mouth and echoed his moan.

His eyes filled with heat, but he didn't say anything. He just turned his attention to his plate, shoveling it in as if he hadn't eaten in days. Honestly, it was a lot like when Cosmo ate his dinner. The dog had never met a meal he didn't love.

Sadie tried to pace herself and was amused when King got up for seconds.

"I could eat an entire vat of this," he said when he sat back down.

"Me, too," she agreed. "I always forget how delicious this is."

"One day, when we're living together, I'm going to request this once a week," he said.

Sadie froze. Did he just say what she thought he'd said? Was he seriously making plans for their future?

When she didn't say anything, he paused and glanced up at her. Then he gave her a slow smile. "You're not freaked out, are you?"

"No," she said automatically. But yes. She was very freaked.

"Sure." He chuckled and went back to his dinner. When they were done, King took their dishes to the kitchen and started loading the dishwasher.

"You don't have to do that," she said as she placed a lid on the glass dish that held the mac and cheese.

He didn't turn around as he said, "You did most of the cooking. I've got this."

Sadie cleaned up the counters and then took Cosmo out. When the pair returned, she found King waiting for her. Without a word, he took one of her hands and led her into the living room. He paused when they reached the couch and brushed a lock of her long hair out of her eyes. "Tell me, Sadie, am I staying or going?"

She raised both eyebrows. "I thought we were going to have a proper make-out session?"

"That's what I wanted to hear." He sat on the couch and then tugged her down so that she was sitting sideways across his lap. Then he kissed her with everything he had, and Sadie decided maybe he'd been onto something when he'd mentioned them living together one day. Because right then, she'd have been content to have him stay forever.

The make-out session went on until Sadie was completely lost in him, and just when she was about to haul him into her bedroom, King pulled back. He was breathless when he said, "I better go."

"Now? Seriously?" She couldn't believe what she was hearing. King McGrath had kissed her senseless for over an hour, and suddenly he was ready to leave when all she could think about was ripping his clothes off? What was wrong with him?

"I have to. If I don't, I'm never going to stop." He looked pained as he got to his feet.

"But—"

He gently placed his fingers to her lips. "Not tonight, Sadie. Not after we wrote an intense song together or after you accepted a date with another man. When we finally take that step, I want it to be after we've chosen each other. Because I promise you that if I had you tonight, there is no way you'd be going to see a band with some guy named *Kasper* tomorrow."

Sadie couldn't help the smile that claimed her lips. She stood and gave him one last kiss before she walked him to the door.

He stepped out onto the porch. "I'll see you tomorrow."

"Probably not tomorrow. I work during the day, and then I have that thing with Melissa. But I'll see you the day after when we rehearse on the stage at the brewery."

"Oh, I'll be there for that. But make no mistake, I'll definitely see you tomorrow." He winked and then took off at a jog toward the black SUV.

As Sadie closed the door, Cosmo came running over. She looked down at him. "What have I gotten myself into?"

Cosmo just blinked up at her.

"Yeah, my thoughts exactly. Come on, boy." She picked him up and headed for the back door. "Let's take you out and get to bed. Tomorrow is going to be a long day."

CHAPTER 11

King took a sip of his beer and watched as Sadie walked around the bar and drew a couple of beers from the tap. He was at the Keating Hollow Brewery with Briggs for dinner even after he'd stopped in at lunch to say hi to Sadie because he'd found out Melissa and Sadie's dates were meeting them there, and he just couldn't resist checking out the guy who was trying to steal his girl.

"Yes!" Melissa cried, taking the beer from Sadie. "Now we can pre-game." She clinked glasses with Sadie, who was still behind the bar, and proceeded to down almost half of her beer.

"Mel, slow down," Sadie insisted. "The night hasn't even started yet." She glanced over at King and Briggs, who were sitting at the bar, and grimaced. "If she gets sloppy, I'll never be able to ditch my date."

"I won't get sloppy!" Melissa cried. "Geez, Sadie. You act like I'm a teenager who's never had a drink before."

"Maybe that's because the last time we went out and started drinking early, I had to help you as you prayed to the porcelain god all night," Sadie countered. "One of us has to be sober enough to get the other one home."

King chuckled into his beer, enjoying the hell out of Sadie and her friend. He couldn't remember the last time he'd been so relaxed around anyone other than Briggs.

"Just how many drinks did you have before you lost it?" Briggs asked, eyeing Melissa with amusement.

"I don't know. More than five, less than a dozen?"

Briggs snickered. "You're my kind of girl." He moved down one barstool so that he was sitting right next to Melissa, and the two of them discussed their favorite bar drinks.

Sadie looked at King. "If I send an SOS tonight, will you come save me?"

"I could save you right now," he said as he put his own beer on the bar and gave her what he hoped was a devastating smile. "Just ditch the loser and we'll go to the festival. Maybe get funnel cake and ride the Ferris wheel."

"You're evil, King McGrath. You know that, right?" Sadie asked him as she clutched at her heart. "You know how much I love funnel cake."

"I do." He shrugged as if he wasn't doing his damnedest to win her over. "It's an open-ended offer. Just let me know when and if you want me to sweep you off your feet and carry you out of here like a rom-com hero."

Her lips twitched as she tried to stifle a smile. "A rom-com hero?"

"Yeah," he said. "That would make a statement, right?"

"Definitely." Sadie walked back around the bar and took Briggs's previous seat.

They both glanced at her friend, who was blushing furiously as Briggs was telling her how sexy she looked in

SONG OF THE WITCH

her black dress. Then Briggs reached out and pushed Melissa's dark curls back and said, "If you need any help getting it off later, you know where to find me."

Melissa giggled. "I'll keep that in mind."

Sadie rolled her eyes. "Can you believe this? She's making me be her wingman for this date, and she's over there flirting with Briggs."

"I think it's Briggs flirting with her," King said. Briggs had always been a relentless flirt, so he wasn't at all surprised by the attention he was paying to Melissa. It was just his MO. "You know, it's not too late for me to carry you out of here. But if I have one more beer, we might have some issues."

She chuckled. "I can move under my own steam, thanks."

"Does that mean we're making a break for it?" he asked hopefully.

The door opened and the douche twins walked in. King had a visceral reaction to the men and was tempted to lay his claim to Sadie right then and there. He probably would have if he hadn't thought she'd throw her drink in his face. And she'd be justified. It wasn't for him to say who she went out with. Especially since he and Sadie weren't even formally dating.

But they would be if he had anything to say about it.

Soon. Very soon.

The one with slightly darker hair, that he thought was named Jasper, paused as he looked around, and then he frowned when his gaze landed on Melissa. She had her hand covering Brigg's, and she was laughing so hard she hadn't even noticed her date walk in. Jasper's expression turned annoyed just before he walked right up to them and crossed his arms over his chest. "Melissa?"

"Jasper?" she gasped out and then whipped around so fast King actually winced.

"How does she not have whiplash?" he wondered aloud.

Sadie just shook her head and stared at the remaining twin.

Kasper walked over to her, a big grin on his face. Then he held his hand out like a salesman. "Sadie, it's so wonderful to see you again."

She glanced at it, hesitated just a moment, and then shook his hand. "Hello, Kasper. I hear you're a big fan of Crimson Vamps."

"Not really." He squeezed her hand, holding on longer than was customary.

King cleared his throat.

Sadie pulled her hand away and gestured to King. "Kasper, this is King McGrath. He's… a friend of mine."

Friend. King wanted to protest. To tell this guy to take his beige slacks and his orange sweater vest and get lost. Instead, he nodded at the other man. "It's nice to meet you, Kasper."

See? His media training had kicked in. If it hadn't, it was likely King would have tossed Kasper out of the brewery right on his ass.

"You, too." Kasper offered his hand to King, who took it and couldn't drop the man's clammy hand soon enough.

King shoved his hands into his pockets and asked, "So, Kasper, do you live here in Keating Hollow?"

"No. I've always wanted to, though. A house like Sadie's would be just perfect for me. But for now, I live over on the coast in Eureka."

"A house like Sadie's? Have you been there?" King probed, trying to tamp down the rising jealousy.

"To her house? Oh no," Kasper said with a chuckle. "I looked it up on Google Maps. It's really charming."

"You looked my house up online?" Sadie asked, her voice high pitched. "Why?"

"No reason, really," the tall, too-tanned man said. "Just curious."

King leaned in close to Sadie. "This is how you're going to end up on the missing person's list. You know that, right?"

Sadie glanced at Kasper, who was frowning at his brother for some reason, and then back at King. Her voice was barely a whisper when she said, "Be ready for that SOS."

"You know you can use it now, right?" King asked.

"I can't." She nodded to Melissa, who had just gotten up and was swaying a little on her feet. Hadn't she only had one beer? King glanced at the bar in front of her and noticed it looked like she'd somehow emptied three large beer steins. "I have to babysit," Sadie added.

King wanted to protest but kept his thoughts to himself as Sadie walked over to her friend, and a few moments later, the foursome headed out the door.

King looked at Briggs and noted him staring at the group as they left the brewery. As soon as the door shut, he shook his head at his friend. "You've got a thing for Melissa."

"What? No, I don't," Briggs said, sounding taken aback. "I was just having a friendly conversation. Can't a guy talk to a woman without everyone assuming he only wants one thing?"

"Nope. And I don't think you're just trying to get into her pants. You like her. You can't fool me. I know you better than anyone else," King insisted.

"Maybe just a little bit," Briggs finally admitted.

"Enough to help me disrupt their date?" King asked, giving his friend an innocent look.

Briggs let out a bark of laughter. "I'm in, brother. Those two weasels are toast."

King left some bills on the bar for their dinner and drinks and then led Briggs out into the cool air.

"Where are we headed?" Briggs asked. "Surely not the concert venue. It's at Equinox, right? I'm pretty positive it's sold out. Otherwise, we'd be there, too."

Equinox was a local pub that had also started hosting live performances by up-and-coming bands. On the nights they had concerts, the pub was restricted to only those who'd purchased tickets. King had to admit that he was pretty annoyed he'd missed out on getting tickets for the Crimson Vamps show. After he'd learned Sadie was headed to the show, he'd gone online to check them out, and as far as King was concerned, they were doing something really special. He'd have to remind himself to look for upcoming dates to see them live. "Not the venue," he confirmed. "Not yet anyway. Just follow me."

⁓

AN HOUR LATER, King and Briggs were sitting at an outdoor table in front of The Magic of Pie, a new shop that was open from seven a.m. to midnight every day. And on the street across them were two horseless carriages that had been painted black and decorated with the skeletons of the horses that would normally pull them through the streets. He sent a quick text to Sadie that just said, *Your SOS is right outside Equinox in the form of headless horseman carriages. Meet us out front.*

SONG OF THE WITCH

"This is how we're going to get Sadie and Melissa away from those two losers?" Briggs asked, sounding skeptical.

"Yep! And we're going to be the drivers, despite still having our heads," King said, staring at the carriages. "Think you can handle that, Briggs?"

Briggs glanced at him. "Are you serious? You want me to steer the invisible horses through town while Melissa is in the carriage with that jackass? Is that what you're going to do to crash Sadie's date?"

"Not quite. The carriages mostly guide themselves, so you won't have to worry about that. But if you're there when they climb in, suddenly you've become the third wheel. A very obnoxious one. Understand?"

"Are you sure Sadie and Melissa won't get angry?" Briggs asked, looking more than a little skeptical.

"No idea, but I don't want them to spend any extra time with those bozos, do you? Sadie already doesn't want to be on this date with Kasper, who, by the way, gives creeper vibes. And his brother was far too territorial over a woman he's only gone out with once," King said, itching to go find Sadie even though the crowds had yet to disperse from the concert.

"Okay, I'm in." Briggs took another bite of his pie. "Just let me finish this first."

"You've got about five minutes," King said, checking his watch. "The show is scheduled to end right about now."

Briggs waved him off and went to town on the rest of his pie.

King, on the other hand, had stopped eating. Dread made his skin cold the instant he saw a group of young women he recognized. They were the obnoxious fans who'd been stalking him all over Keating Hollow since word had gotten out that he was in town. King stood abruptly, looking both ways, trying to find a spot that would hide him from the stalker fans.

But there wasn't one. Not in Keating Hollow, which had a Main Street and just a couple of other services on the outside of town.

"Oh. My. Goddess! It's King McGrath!" a woman called, and King cursed. There was literally nowhere to go to get away from them. He stood frozen by the realization that he was going to get mobbed again. *No, not tonight,* he thought. Not when he was busy interrupting a date some guy had with his girl.

The doors to the concert hall burst open, and people started to stumble out. He wanted to look for Sadie, but there was no time. The fans were already upon him, forming a circle as if to trap him in their bubble.

He made a break for it, running full speed toward the horseless carriage. The women were chasing behind him, calling out for autographs as one declared her undying love. King dove headfirst into the first carriage and landed right on top of someone's lap. He glanced up into the surprised face of Sadie's date, Kasper.

"Oof," King said, rolling off the man and onto the floor of the carriage.

"King?" Sadie cried, suddenly right beside him, rubbing her hands all over him as though looking for broken bones or signs of injury.

The carriage had already started moving, and the crazed fans were running after it.

King just closed his eyes and tried to pretend it wasn't happening. But it was useless. He could hear them screaming his name and shouting hysterically, and it unnerved him. He sat up and ran a hand through his hair.

"Dude," Kasper said, looking wistfully at all the groupies still trying to chase down the carriage. "Does this happen a lot?"

"Far more often than I'd like," he said, more to Sadie than the loser who appeared to be enthralled by the mob of women still running behind them.

"Your life is so cool," Kasper said, sounding like a major jackass.

"Oh. Em. Gee!" Sadie exclaimed as she stood and pointed a finger at Kasper. "You are the worst. Can't you see that King doesn't want to be harassed or followed? All he wants is —" She looked at King, seemingly hesitant to finish that statement.

He stood up and draped an arm over her shoulder, pulling her to him. "Peace and quiet sounds perfect. The only thing that would make it better is alone time with my girl."

Kasper narrowed his eyes and clamped his lips together in a tight line. "You're manhandling my date."

"So? You were borrowing my girl for the night. Neither of us are happy," King said calmly and then snapped his fingers. Both carriages stopped abruptly near the end of Main Street. King turned to Kasper. "It's the end of the line."

"What?"

"Time to go. This ride is over," King said, trying to ignore the catcalls still filling the air. He was tired of this loser. He wanted Sadie all to himself.

Kasper looked at Sadie, frowned, and then shook his head as he jumped out of the carriage. As he started walking away, he muttered something about shallow girls.

"I'm *not* shallow," Sadie called, her expression beyond irritated.

King agreed and pulled her back into his arms. "Now we can start the carriage tour and maybe end the night with funnel cake."

"I'm in." Sadie smiled up at him and then stared at his lips as she started to lean in.

Just as King lowered his lips to hers, they heard an *oomph* and cries of distress from the carriage just behind them. King spun, ready to jump into action to help Briggs and Melissa defend against whoever had attacked them. But what he saw made him laugh until tears streamed down his face.

Briggs was standing at the edge of the carriage, glaring down at Jasper, who happened to be lying on top of three of the fans who'd still been chasing them.

"Don't ever talk to a woman like that," Briggs ordered. "Or I'll do a lot worse than kick your ass out of a carriage."

Melissa was standing behind Briggs, scowling at Jasper. "And keep your damned hands to yourself."

Sadie stood next to King, taking in the scene. Her body was rigid as if she were on high alert. But as Melissa flipped off Jasper, Sadie's shoulders started to shake with her laughter. Finally, she gasped out, "Serves them right."

CHAPTER 12

After the twins had been ejected from the carriages, Sadie settled into the carriage seat with King at her side.

He wrapped an arm around her shoulders and tugged her in close. "How was that for an SOS?"

"Perfect." Sadie relaxed with a contented sigh. "You would not believe what I had to endure throughout the entire concert." She felt King stiffen beside her, and she quickly said, "Nothing you need to go all caveman over."

"Well, that's a relief. What did the jackass do?"

"Good ole Kasper asked me what I thought of his outfit, and when I was noncommittal, he said his mother picked it out for him," Sadie said, shaking her head.

"Uh, what? His mother came over to help him get dressed for his date?"

"Oh, no. The doofus twins live with their mother," Sadie said with a soft chuckle. "She apparently does almost everything for them, so I got to listen to him talk about how much he wanted to get married and how he's so progressive because he likes to clean. Especially mopping and controlling the robot vacuum. The man has a serious fetish for those things."

"That's super weird," King said.

"Yep. But I shouldn't worry, because he fully supports my prerogative to quit my job and homeschool the kids."

King sat up and stared at her. "This is a joke, right?"

Sadie laughed as she shook her head. "Nope. Apparently, he googled my house because he wanted to make sure it had potential as a family home. It wasn't a deal breaker, but he wanted to know up front before we got serious."

"I'm guessing if I hadn't kicked him off the carriage, you'd have done it yourself the moment you had a chance," King said as he settled back down and pulled her back into his arms.

"He's lucky I didn't kick him in the nuts." It had been damned close, but somehow Sadie had managed to control herself for Melissa's sake. If for some reason it had worked out between her and Jasper, Sadie didn't want to have drama between her and Jasper's family.

King let out a bark of laughter that made her grin up at him.

Sadie glanced back at the carriage behind them and spotted Melissa chatting animatedly with Briggs. "Looks like those two are getting along."

"I wouldn't read too much into it," King said, trying to curb her expectation. "Briggs is a shameless flirt, but I've never seen him serious about anyone."

"Ah, he's one of those, is he? Well, Melissa is a serial dater, so they are probably a decent match... for now."

The rest of the evening was spent admiring the Halloween decorations that covered practically the entire

SONG OF THE WITCH

town. Sadie's favorite was a large Victorian house that overlooked the river that had animated gargoyles on the roof, ghostly figures in the windows, and a light show with bats that flew in a formation that was coordinated to the song "Thriller" by Michael Jackson.

By the time the carriage pulled up in front of her house, she'd almost forgotten all about the twins.

King hopped out of the carriage and then held his hand out to her.

"Such a gentleman," she said as she climbed down. "Thank you for salvaging my evening."

"It was my pleasure." King started to guide her to her door, but Sadie pointed to the house next to hers.

"I'm at Melissa's for the next couple of weeks," Sadie said. "There's a termite infestation at my place, so tomorrow it's getting tented bright and early for a few days. Once they take the tent down, they're working on rebuilding my porch and fixing the foundation. Melissa graciously offered us her spare room."

"Termites? That sounds bad," King said.

"It's not good," she agreed, desperately wishing the work on her house wasn't starting the next day. She'd give anything to invite King into her house. Ask him to stay over. To finally find out what it was like to be with *the* King McGrath.

But that would have to wait for another day. When she spotted Briggs waving at Melissa as she hurried up to her front door, Sadie knew it was time to say goodnight to King.

"Thank you for the save and the lovely carriage ride. It really salvaged an otherwise horrible evening," she said.

"Anytime, Sadie Lewis. Just send that SOS." King dipped

99

his head and gave her a sweet kiss and then climbed back into the carriage.

She stood on the curb, watching as the two men rolled away in the horseless carriages. When they turned the corner, she finally went into Melissa's house, let Cosmo out, and then went to find her friend.

"Mel?" Sadie called as she and Cosmo headed down the hallway toward her friend's bedroom. "Are you back here?"

"Yes." The moment Sadie walked into her bedroom, Melissa asked, "Can you believe how awful that date was? Who could have guessed that Jasper would be such a creep?"

Me, Sadie thought. At least judging by his brother. That man had no concept of boundaries. Who searched online for their date's address and then googled their house with the idea that he'd be living in it some day? Her skin was still crawling after learning that tidbit. But after he'd been so unceremoniously dismissed, Sadie guessed she wouldn't have to worry about seeing him again. "I'm sorry it didn't work out," Sadie lied. "But it looks like you had a fun time with Briggs at least."

Melissa walked over to her closet and pulled out her suitcase. She was going out of town for business in the morning and would be gone for a few days. She was a sales rep for a number of wineries up and down the California coast, including the Pelsh winery. "Briggs is fun. And I grilled him about King for you."

"Mel!" Sadie picked up Cosmo and the two of them sat down on her friend's bed. "I didn't need you to do that."

"I know, but if I don't look after you, who will?" She smiled sweetly at her friend. "Besides, after that fiasco tonight, I wanted to make sure you weren't hanging out with another jackass. Briggs says he's got some baggage but is a decent guy. So I guess I approve of whatever you two have going on."

Baggage was an understatement. But who didn't have at least some baggage? Goddess knew that Sadie had more than her fair share.

Melissa pulled out a pretty dress and held up a pair of white ankle boots. "Do these go together?"

"Sure."

"Oh, good. I always wonder what shoes to wear once it starts getting chilly. It was either these or my six-inch heels, and those just seem so impractical." Melissa went on to babble about five or six more of her outfits she was considering for her trip until finally Sadie held her hand up, stopping her.

"I know what you're doing," Sadie said.

"And what's that?" she asked, paying extra attention to the socks she was placing in her suitcase.

"You're babbling so we don't have to talk about Jasper. Or his creepy brother Kasper. We should have known they were bad news with names like that," Sadie added, trying to keep it light.

"Eh, what's to talk about? You didn't like Kasper from the start, and I guilted you into going. And then it turns out that Jasper was just a bully. A true asshole when he didn't get his way. All I have to say is good riddance."

Sadie reached over and covered her friend's hand with her own. "Are you sure you're okay?"

"Yeah. I'll be all right. He's not the first total jerk I've dated. At least I didn't waste weeks on him, right?" Her tone was resigned, but then she seemed to perk up when she said, "It's all good. Now I'm free to jump Briggs. That man is one gorgeous specimen."

"Something tells me he'll have no problem with that," Sadie said with a chuckle. She put Cosmo on the floor and then went to hug her friend. "I love you."

"Love you, too, sweetie." She stepped back. "Now get out of here so I can finish packing. If you're not up when I leave in the morning, I'll see you in a few days."

"You'll be back for our performance, right?" Sadie asked, suddenly worried her main person might not be there.

"I wouldn't miss it for the world." Melissa bent down to give Cosmo pets and said, "Take care of your mama for me."

He gave Melissa an enthusiastic tail wag before following Sadie to their room.

～

THE SUN WAS STREAMING through the window when Sadie finally opened her eyes the next morning. She groaned her displeasure and blinked rapidly until her eyes adjusted.

"Cosmo?" she said, looking around the room for her pup. He wasn't next to her where he usually slept, nor was he in his dog bed. But her bedroom door was cracked open, so she assumed that Melissa had let him out.

She rolled out of bed and padded into the kitchen. The moment she opened the refrigerator door, Cosmo came running in from the living room. He jumped excitedly as he barked his good mornings.

"Hey, buddy. Did your Auntie Melissa already leave?" she asked him.

Cosmo ran around in circles, too excited by the morning to relax.

Chuckling to herself, she went in search of coffee. While it was brewing, she found the note that Melissa had left letting her know that Cosmo had been out and she'd fed him breakfast.

"Thanks, Mel," Sadie said to the void while she got her coffee. With her mug in hand, Sadie headed to the bathroom, ready to get her day started. She'd only got as far as brushing her teeth when she heard an ominous gurgling sound coming from the pipes.

Just as she turned, the sound was even louder, followed by brown sludge that spurted out of the drain, filling the tub. The sewer scent made her gag, and she ran out of the bathroom and into Melissa's bathroom only to find the same sludge in her shower.

"Holy hell!" Sadie cried as she ran back into the kitchen, looking for her phone.

An hour later, the sewage had only backed up further and Sadie was sitting outside with Cosmo as a serviceman inspected the septic. When he finally appeared, his face was grim. "Your friend has tree roots blocking her pipes. There are multiple sections that need to be replaced, and her septic needs repairs. It won't be cheap, and unfortunately it won't be today. We can pump out the sewage, but she can't use the plumbing until we can get back to get the work done."

Sadie's heart sank as she looked over at her house, which was already tented and being fumigated. "How long will it be until you can get back?"

"Three, four days, tops. We can try for sooner, but there's no guarantee. I suggest finding somewhere else to stay for a few days." He tore off the estimate and handed Sadie his business card. "Have your friend call us to authorize the work, and we'll get it scheduled right away."

"I will." Sadie took the paperwork and called Melissa to give her the bad news.

CHAPTER 13

"Hey, isn't that Sadie?" Briggs said as he and King walked out of Incantation Café.

King followed his gaze and there she was. Sadie was sitting at one of the outside tables with Cosmo lying at her feet. Just looking at her suddenly made him feel lighter. He didn't hesitate as he walked up to her table and sat across from her. "Is this seat taken?"

Sadie glanced up, clearly startled before she gave him a tired smile. "It is now." She glanced at Briggs and nodded at the remaining chair. "What are you two up to today?"

"Hanging with you." Briggs winked at her.

"Not if you want to have any fun today," she said with a sigh. Cosmo noticed and nudged her hand until she picked him up and put him in her lap. He snuggled into her chest, loving on her.

"What's wrong, Sadie?" King asked, frowning. "It doesn't have anything to do with the douche twins, does it? They didn't try to get in touch with you, did they?"

"Oh, no." She laughed at his description before she closed

her eyes for just a moment. "Nothing like that. Remember I told you that my house is being tented and fumigated?"

"Yeah." King hoped they hadn't found more problems. He knew how much she loved that house.

"Well, I was supposed to be staying at Melissa's, but it turns out she has plumbing issues, and I can't stay there until they get it fixed. So Cosmo and I are homeless at the moment. I've been looking for a short-term rental here in Keating Hollow, but there's nothing except this six-bedroom estate due to all the tourists in town for the harvest festival. There's a room at the inn, but I can't leave Cosmo there because he'll bark all day if he hears a noise. So now I'm looking at getting something at the coast and commuting every day, but then Cosmo will be locked up too long all day because I won't be able to run home to let him out. And now I'm just totally frustrated." She hugged Cosmo to her and gave him a kiss on his head.

"Damn," King said. "That's awful."

She nodded, looking miserable. "If it wasn't for the holiday, this wouldn't be that big of a deal. I'd still take a hit to my pocketbook, but that's what credit cards are for, right?" Sadie started typing one-handed on the laptop in front of her. "Maybe I can find a doggie day care for this guy." She grimaced and mumbled, "My poor credit card."

Briggs reached out and tugged the computer away from Sadie. "Forget doggie daycare or staying on the coast. Both of you can stay with us at my place."

Sadie stared at him blankly as if she hadn't quite processed what he'd said. Then she suddenly shook her head. "No. I couldn't do that. Thank you, but I can't put you out like that."

"You're not putting him out," King said, vowing to buy his

buddy a month's worth of beer. "He has a third unused bedroom just sitting there."

"It's true," Briggs said with a smile. "I have visions of one day turning it into a home recording studio, but I just haven't gotten around to it yet. It's okay to say yes, Sadie. The mattress is new. Never even been slept on. Come stay and help me feel like I didn't waste my money creating a guest room when I never have guests."

Sadie glanced at King. "Isn't he a guest?"

"King?" Briggs threw his head back and laughed. "Nope. Never a guest. My house is his house. And he bought his own bedroom furniture. So at least I didn't have to buy three beds when I moved in."

King gave his friend a grateful smile and echoed his encouragement. "It's a gift to let your friends who care about you help when they can. It really is okay to say yes."

Sadie's eyes clouded with tears as she nodded. "Okay. Yes. Thank you, Briggs. You're really saving me here. But please let me pay you some sort of rent. You'll have me and Cosmo, and you have no idea what you're getting into."

"No way." Briggs stood. "Not taking your money. Just return the favor sometime or pass it on when you can."

"I can't pay nothing," Sadie insisted.

King refrained from rolling his eyes at her. He understood her need to be independent, to not take charity from anyone. It was normal for people who had their type of childhood trauma to overcompensate by assuming they had to do everything for themselves. He hadn't exactly taken Briggs up on his free room right away either. But his friend had insisted, saying they were brothers and the only family they each had. He wasn't taking no for an answer. It had been the best decision King had made in a while. Spending time with Briggs helped him feel connected. Like he belonged there. And that was something he desperately needed.

"How about a barter?" King asked Sadie. "Instead of paying rent, you could cook for us."

"Us?" Briggs said, raising an eyebrow. Then he laughed. "Last I checked, your name isn't on the deed."

This time King did roll his eyes. "How about I help Sadie with the dinners then? I'll be the sous chef."

"I'll gladly make dinners for you guys," Sadie said. "I love to cook. So in exchange for a room here in Keating Hollow, all I need to do is keep your bellies full?"

"No. You don't need to do anything," Briggs said. "But if you cook, I'll eat it."

"Good. It's a deal," Sadie said, looking more relaxed and content than she had all morning.

Briggs pulled out his keyring and loosened a key. He put it right by her coffee cup and said, "The key to the house and garage. Go over any time you want. I have to be in the studio for a few hours this afternoon, so I won't be there to show you around."

"I can do it," King said as he rose from his chair. "How about we go now so you can get Cosmo settled, and then we can talk about dinner."

Sadie put Cosmo down and then rose and threw her arms around Briggs. "Thank you. You're saving my life."

"Anytime, Sadie," Briggs said. "Anytime."

CHAPTER 14

"I brought groceries!" Sadie called as she got out of her car and retrieved Cosmo from his doggie seat. She glanced up at the cheerful yellow house that sat surrounded by redwoods and smiled. The craftsman had a wide window in front that overlooked the charming front porch. But what she liked the most was the second story sunroom that looked to be an addition to the attic. She could just imagine Briggs and King up there working on music.

"You didn't have to do that," King said, bounding off the porch to come help her unload her car.

"It's the least I can do," she said and popped the trunk open.

Cosmo ran toward King, his tail wagging and his tongue out.

King stopped to give the dog love before he grabbed her grocery bags.

"I think you've made a friend for life," Sadie said. "Usually it takes Cosmo a little longer to warm up to people."

"He just has good taste. He picked you, didn't he?"

Sadie laughed. "Okay, I can go with that." She grabbed her suitcase, closed the trunk, and followed King into the house.

After King dropped off the groceries, he led her to her room. "Make yourself at home. I'll put your groceries away."

"Thanks," she said as he retreated. Once he was gone, Sadie hauled her suitcase onto the bed and looked at Cosmo. "We lucked out, boy."

He jumped up, putting his paws on the side of the bed, making her shake her head.

"You're a handful, you know that, right?" The moment she put him on the bed, he curled up next to the pillow and closed his eyes. No doubt he was worn out from all the activity of the day.

Ten minutes later, with Cosmo fast asleep on the bed, Sadie made her way to the kitchen, where she found King sitting at the counter, frowning at his phone. "Something wrong?"

He glanced up at her, frustration in his expression. "No. I don't think so."

She raised her eyebrows at him. "You don't think so?"

"It's my mother. She keeps calling, and I keep ignoring her because she's mad that I won't fund her new Lexus. But…" He shook his head. "She just sent a text saying they are being evicted and will be homeless by the end of the month."

Sadie took a seat next to him. "I take it you're not sure if you should believe her."

"You got it." He closed his eyes and took in a deep breath. "She only gets in touch when she wants money. Earlier this week it was money for a car after the one she had was totaled. I sent enough for a decent used car, but she wasn't happy. And now she's saying this."

"And the problem is you don't trust her," Sadie said as she reached across the table to squeeze his hand. "It's a rough position to be in."

King flipped his hand over and then entwined his fingers with hers. "I hate this."

"I know."

He cursed under his breath and picked up the phone with his free hand. Sadie was silent as he tapped the screen, making a call.

"Kevin. Finally!" his mom said so loudly that Sadie had no trouble hearing her. "What is so important that you couldn't call your mother back for a week?"

King rose from the stool and started to pace the kitchen. "What's going on? Why are you being evicted?"

Sadie could hear his mother talking but couldn't make out the details. But as he continued to listen, King's expression turned more and more stormy. Anger flashed in his dark blue eyes as he scowled.

Finally, King said, "Did you just threaten to go to the press and blame me for your poor financial decisions?"

The press? Sadie was horrified for King. What she'd heard about his parents was nightmare fuel.

"That's blackmail, Mother." King seethed.

Sadie wanted to tell him to end the call. To change his number. Put out a press release that he was divorced from the people who rejected him as a kid. Instead, she sat on her stool, fuming and desperate to make sure he knew that there were at least a couple of people in his life who were only interested in him for *him*, not what he could do for them.

"Give me the landlord's number, and I'll take care of it. But this is the last time, Mother. I'm done being the family bank account," King said.

"Just send me the money, Kevin!" his mother screamed into the phone. "I can handle the landlord."

"No," King said, shaking his head. "I'm done sending you money. If you really need this money for rent, I'll pay your landlord directly. Take it or leave it."

There was silence on the other end of the connection.

A few seconds passed until King pulled the phone away from his ear and looked at the screen. "I guess she didn't like my terms," he said as he tossed his phone onto the table.

"She hung up on you?" Sadie asked, stunned by what she'd just witnessed.

"Yep."

King looked so dejected, almost broken. Sadie didn't think, she just moved and wrapped him in her arms, holding him close. He clung to her, his body trembling, and Sadie tightened her hold on him, wanting to fill him up with the love she had for him.

They held each other until King finally pulled back and wiped at his eyes. "Sorry. I just…"

"You don't need to explain." Sadie took his hand in hers and led him into the living room. They sat together on the couch, their hands clasped. Sadie turned to him and gently brushed a lock of his dark curls back. "They don't deserve you."

He nodded, staring down at their joined hands. "I know." Then he looked up at her, his expression troubled. "How do I know if I'm handling this right?"

Sadie grimaced. "I'm not sure I'm the one to ask. I don't deal with my father at all. Not after everything that went down back in Salem."

He looked at her curiously. "Do you mind telling me about it?"

Normally Sadie didn't talk about her father. She preferred to pretend that he didn't even exist. But in that moment, she knew if she shared her story that King would feel less alone. "Are you sure you want to hear this now?"

He nodded, giving her hand a slight squeeze.

"Okay. Well, you already know that he showed up and forced me to go Back East with him, which I did not want to do. When my grandmother realized she couldn't fight it, she moved there, too. At least I had her, though she couldn't afford my father's neighborhood and got a house a couple of towns over." Sadie's voice caught as tears stung her eyes. She blinked them back as she added, "She died two weeks after she got there. They said it was a stroke. I think it was the stress of what happened with my father."

"Oh, Sadie," King said. "I'm so sorry. I had no idea."

She nodded and did her best to work past the pain that throbbed in her chest. "My father, who took me out to Salem because he was supposedly so concerned with us being a family, refused to let me go to her service. He said I needed to settle in and get to know my stepmother."

"Was she terrible, too?" King asked.

"No, actually. I rather liked Sherry. She was a sweet woman who didn't deserve the way my father treated her. It didn't take me long to recognize that my father was all about appearances. He literally made me leave my grandmother because he wanted me to date the son of a powerful developer so that he would have an inside track to get a meeting with him."

"He did *what?*" King stood suddenly, staring down at Sadie in horror. "Your father was pimping you out?"

"Not quite." Sadie shook her head. "It's not like he wanted me to sleep with the son. He just wanted me to date him long enough for my father to gain access to his dad. Everything Sherry and I were expected to do always revolved around connections and business deals. He used us both when he needed a respectable family to show off. When he didn't, he ignored us."

Sadie got up and took King's hands in hers. "It was ten months of living with a selfish narcissist, and the final straw was when he tried to sell my mom's house without telling me. He had it on the market and even had a buyer. I found out about it when Melissa's mom, Rachel, called to make sure that was what I wanted. She was the executor of Mom's estate. If it hadn't been for her, I'd have lost my mom's house, and my dad would have taken the money. Rachel refused to let the sale go through, even though my dad hired lawyers and threatened to bankrupt the estate if she wouldn't do what he wanted."

"Your dad sounds like my mom," King said, his voice flat and emotionless.

"Yeah, they aren't far apart in their ruthlessness to use their own children for personal gain. Pretty disgusting." She gave him a sad smile. "I'm sorry to say that I completely understand that ball of rage inside of you that is covered in a healthy layer of guilt because you're not doing what they want you to."

"So, you do know how I'm feeling." He laughed suddenly. "Except you ran away and I was kicked out. We're quite the pair, aren't we?"

"Bonding over trauma. It's what we do best." She winked at him.

He nodded and then sat back down on the couch and leaned back, staring up at her. "So how am I supposed to deal with this now? She won't let me just pay her rent to the landlord. She says that will make her look unstable, and she won't have her son meddling in her affairs. I'm supposed to just transfer the money to her, or she's going to sell her story to a tabloid."

"Sell what story? That she kicked you out, making you homeless?" Sadie gasped out.

"No, the one that says her celebrity son won't help his struggling family," he said bitterly.

"Holy hell." Sadie flopped down next to him on the couch. "I don't know, King. I haven't had to deal with celebrity stuff. I don't have a reputation to protect, so I just ignore my father. He's been cut out of my life. If he started threatening me now, I suppose I'd have to get a lawyer."

"And a PR person," King said, sounding resigned now. "If I keep giving her money, she's never going to leave me alone."

"I'm sure that's true." Sadie felt lucky that at least her father didn't have money issues. If he did, she was certain he'd try the same kind of garbage with her if he got wind she was having any success. However, she was confident that he wouldn't want any kind of scandal following him around, so the idea that he'd sell a story to the tabloids was laughable.

"But if I don't continue to help her financially, my past is going to be splashed all over the gossip sites." He ground his teeth together.

"I wish I could wave a wand and make this all go away for you," she said. "Celebrity seems pretty awful if you ask me. Between your mother's BS and those groupies, I don't know how you deal with it."

He glanced over at her. "You do realize that once our song is out in the world it's very likely you'll end up dealing with similar stuff, right?"

Sadie just raised both hands palms up. "You and Austin keep saying that the song is going to be a hit, but it's hard for me to imagine that. It's not real to me."

Chuckling, King pulled her close and gave her a soft kiss. "It's going to be very real. I think maybe both of us need to see a PR person tomorrow. Right after I call my lawyer."

"Does this mean your mom is cut off?"

He nodded. "It's what I have to do, even if I have to book an interview to set the record straight. I can't keep letting her use me like this."

Sadie reached over and pressed her hand to his heart. "You're a good man, King McGrath. No matter what your mother or anyone in the media says. You remember that, okay?"

He caught her hand with his and brought it to his lips, giving her palm a kiss. "I will."

CHAPTER 15

Usually after King spoke with his mother, it put him in a funk for days. But having Sadie nearby to talk to had given him some much-needed perspective. After hearing her story about how her father tried to sell her house right from underneath her, he'd been horrified. And had he been the one giving her advice about her father, he'd have told her to cut him off immediately and press charges if at all possible.

But why had he never done that with his mother? Why had he let that guilt keep creeping in? She hadn't done anything that had helped him in achieving success. In fact, she and his father had actively harmed him as a teen, making it even harder for him to get a start in the music business.

It was impossible to try to write songs and play music when one was fighting for food and shelter every day. And because he and Briggs had left their foster home with almost nothing, that's exactly all they'd had for a few years until they finally had stable jobs and a safe apartment. It was only then that he'd been able to concentrate on bettering his craft.

He knew it was time to break the cycle with his mother. He just hoped he was ready for the shitstorm that would follow.

"Come on," Sadie said, getting up off the couch and tugging him with her. "Let's go work on dinner. Do you think Briggs will be home soon?"

"I'm not sure," King said as he followed her to the kitchen. "Let me ask him." Just as King grabbed his phone from the table, Brigg's picture flashed on the screen with an incoming call. "Hey, brother. Are you on your way? Sadie's cooking."

"No, that's what I called about. I've got plans tonight," Briggs said, sounding distracted. "Don't be surprised if I don't make it home."

"Hot date?" King asked with a chuckle. "Or just a hookup?"

"Not sure yet. Gotta go."

The call ended, and King looked over at Sadie, who was busy pulling food out of the refrigerator. "Briggs is a no show tonight."

Sadie spun around to face him. "Really? That's too bad. I was going to make a huge lasagna, but it will be too much for just us."

King walked over to her and grabbed the cheese out of her hands. He quickly put it back in the fridge and said, "I have a better idea."

"Oh, you're cooking?" she asked, her right dimple showing as she grinned at him.

"No, but I do plan to feed you. Do you like sushi?"

"Who doesn't?" she asked as if that was a given.

"Good, cause if you're up for it, I'd like to take you on a date." King's heart was beating too fast, and he wondered if he'd ever been this nervous asking someone out before. He

SONG OF THE WITCH

highly doubted it. "What do you say to a beachside dinner and a walk in the moonlight over at the coast?"

"You want to take me to the beach tonight?" Sadie asked, clearly a little shellshocked.

"Yes."

"And I don't have to cook," she said, more to herself as if she were mulling over the offer.

"Nope." Damn, he couldn't help but be amused by her.

"Okay, but I'm making lasagna tomorrow night, and you tell Briggs his presence is required. Got it?"

King gave her a mock salute. "Got it. Now go find some clothes appropriate for the beach."

Sadie grinned at him and hurried off to her room.

Twenty minutes later, after Cosmo had been taken out and fed dinner, Sadie met him at the door. "I'm ready."

"Sadie Lewis," he said as he took her hand, "I've been waiting for this for ten years."

∽

"THAT WAS the best sushi I've ever had," Sadie declared as they walked out of the restaurant. "How did you hear about this place?"

King wrapped his hand around hers, marveling that the gesture had become almost second nature already. Every time he touched her, it just felt *right*. And he was starting to think their hands had magnets in them because they couldn't keep them off each other. "Briggs. We came here a few weeks ago. It's kind of a hidden gem."

"I'd say it's a lot more than kind of; it was perfect." She stopped suddenly and planted a sweet kiss on his lips.

But King wanted more from her. He pulled her in closer

until their bodies were molded together and said, "Are you ready for a proper kiss?"

"Proper kiss. Hmm, sounds interesting," she said, staring at his mouth. "Don't keep me waiting, King."

"Never." He yanked her closer still and then claimed her lips, kissing her with the intention of making her head spin. She tasted of soy sauce and sake and something sweet that was unique to her. His body responded instantly, and if they hadn't been standing in front of the restaurant, he'd have shown her exactly how much he wanted her.

When he finally broke the kiss, Sadie didn't move. She just stood there, breathless as she held her fingertips to her lips.

"Sadie?" he asked with a chuckle. "You all right?"

A slow smile claimed her lips as she stared into his eyes. "Better than all right. Now take me to the beach. I'm ready to relive my teenage years."

"Good, because that's exactly what I had planned." King winked at her before leading her to the car.

The beach access parking lot was deserted except for one lone truck that was parked all the way at the end of the lot.

"Looks like we have the beach to ourselves," Sadie said as she jumped out of his white Jeep.

"I guess not a lot of people are interested at the end of October," King said, pulling a blanket and a lantern out of the back. "They aren't hardcore like we are."

Sadie snorted her amusement. "I'm not sure I'd call us hardcore. Maybe just a little sentimental."

King ran his fingers over the small box he'd put in his pocket earlier and said, "Definitely sentimental."

It wasn't nearly as cold on the beach as King had feared. They'd gotten lucky. The cloud cover had trapped some heat from the day, and there was almost no wind, a rarity for the beach.

Sadie opened her arms wide and then let out a cry of joy as she ran full speed toward the water. King had a sudden flashback of her at seventeen when she'd done the exact same thing, and all he could think about was how happy he'd been that day, watching her come alive after suffering from the pain and loss of her mother. It was the day he'd completely fallen head over heels for her.

"Come on, slowpoke!" she called. "You're missing it."

King jogged toward her, and when he got to her side, he asked, "Missing what?"

"There are a couple of seals right there. You can see their heads bobbing in the moonlight. See 'em?"

"Sure," he lied, but only because he couldn't take his eyes off her. Sadie was radiant in the moonlight when the clouds parted. Full of wonder and life. This was what he'd missed. Their time together. The way her energy had always been infectious. She made him feel lighter and freer just by existing. He'd known it was special then, but now he knew it was something incredibly rare, and he decided he'd be damned if he ever let her go again.

"Why are you staring at me?" she asked, shaking her head, though she didn't look upset.

"You would be too if you could see yourself in this moonlight."

Sadie scoffed and then chuckled to herself. "Okay, now you're just laying it on a little thick. Here's a tip, King McGrath; you don't have to try so hard with me. I already like you."

"That's good. Cause I like you, too." He wrapped his arm

around her shoulders and said, "Walk with me. I want to show you something."

King and Briggs had been to this beach a couple of times since King had come to town. He was a beach lover at heart. Almost all of his happiest memories had happened while at the beach. It's where he'd met Sadie and fallen for her. It was also where he and Briggs had spent a lot of their free time while in the foster home and then later when they moved to LA. The surf, sand, and sun had been free and had always calmed his nerves. It was also where he did some of his best songwriting. There was just something about the pull of the ocean that spoke to him.

"Show me something, huh? It's not your…" She glanced down at his groin and then met his eyes again.

"My what, Sadie?" he asked innocently.

"Oh, shut up. You know what I mean. Your package. Okay? You didn't bring me all the way out here just for that, did you? Because there seem to be perfectly good beds back at Briggs's house." Her eyes widened, and she clamped a hand over her mouth, clearly regretting voicing those thoughts out loud.

King threw his head back and laughed.

"Okay, that's enough laughing at me," she said. "I just meant that sand in unusual places isn't all that sexy."

"But I brought a blanket," King said innocently, blinking down at her.

"Good luck with that."

He was still chuckling when they came upon an outcropping of rocks. "This is what I wanted to show you."

Sadie stared at it and then at him. "Is there a little hidden cove on the other side?"

He nodded.

"You're kidding!" she cried and started to run again.

This time King kept pace with her, and when they rounded the largest outcropping, they both stopped suddenly, taking in the small cove. It reminded him so much of the one where they used to meet in Westhaven.

"It's perfect." Sadie stepped right in front of him and reached up with both hands, placing them to either side of his face. "You are amazing." Then she was the one kissing him within an inch of his life.

Once she pulled away, he caught his breath and then leaned his forehead against hers. "Careful, Sadie. At this rate, you really will see my package right here on the beach."

"I'm not sure that'd be a bad thing," Sadie said, fanning herself. Damn, that man was hot.

"Even with the sand issue?" he teased.

"It is a problem," Sadie agreed. "However, I'm sure that if we're creative, we can find a way to make it work."

King laid the blanket out on the sand and wished he'd thought to bring candles to make it a little bit more special. But at least he had the electric lantern. He flipped it on and decided it would do. "Care to join me?" King asked from his place on the blanket.

"I'd be happy to." Sadie took her spot on the blanket and then turned to him. "Should I be taking my shoes off?"

"Only if you want to," he said.

Sadie shook her head before snuggling in next to him. "Not tonight. It's starting to get chillier."

Was it? He hadn't even noticed. He was too busy thinking about the box in his pocket.

"King, what's wrong? You look... I don't know, like maybe you ate some bad sushi."

Did he? That wasn't good. "It's not the sushi," he said as

the clouds parted and the moonlight beamed down on them. "But I do have something to ask you, and I might be a tad nervous."

Sadie curled her legs up under her as she gave King her full attention.

"It's just me. You don't need to be nervous," she reassured him.

But then he pulled a small black box out of his pocket and started to open it. His hands were shaking slightly, and he was starting to feel like a fool. This was too soon. What had he been thinking? He should have given her some space and time before *this*.

"King? What's happening right now?" Sadie asked, suddenly sounding just as nervous as he felt.

"What should have happened ten years ago but didn't because of your father." He cleared his throat. "I've been holding onto this pendant for a decade. I bought it the day we were supposed to play at that club. The day your father made you leave Westhaven."

"Pendant?" she asked in a timid but hopeful voice.

"Yeah. Pendant," he said. "It's supposed to be blessed with luck, love, and prosperity. I wanted you to have it as a promise of what was to come in our future… together."

"Together?" she repeated. "King McGrath, is this some sort of promise pendant?"

He ran his fingertips lightly over her jawline. "It is if you want it to be."

She hesitated for a long moment and then grinned as she took the pendant out of the box and said, "Yes."

CHAPTER 16

"Are you ready?" King asked Sadie when she walked out of her room with Cosmo on her heels.

"No," she said with a nervous laugh. "I don't think I'm ever going to be ready for this." Sadie took a moment to really look at King. He was wearing jeans that did wonders for his backside and a Henley that clung to his well-defined torso, along with black motorcycle boots. And with the way his curls were styled to give him a controlled messy look, he was every inch a rock star. "You look hot."

He grinned at her. "Right back at you, gorgeous."

Sadie flushed. She'd opted for a formfitting V-neck T-shirt that showed off all her curves with a plaid miniskirt and knee-high black boots. She felt a little silly, but Melissa had assured her that she'd look amazing on stage, so she'd just gone with it and hoped for the best. Considering it was Halloween night, Sadie figured she and King were probably going to be the most normal looking people at the festival. But when one was trying to be a rock star, she figured it was best to look the part.

What was that saying? Dress for the job you want? Well, she was doing her best rock star impersonation. She'd just have to hope for the best. After the night at the beach, Sadie felt as if she'd been living in some sort of dream. She felt seventeen again, giddy with happiness about being with King. After they'd gotten back from the beach that night, they'd spent a lot of time making out on the couch until Briggs stumbled in, interrupting them. Apparently his sleepover hadn't panned out.

He'd been more than a little drunk, but thankfully had taken a rideshare home, and after that, King had spent the entire night taking care of him.

Sadie had left him to it, assuring him that she understood. She'd spent her share of nights taking care of Melissa after having one too many and vice versa.

But it had meant that their evening had been cut short, and Sadie's plans of dragging him to her bedroom never materialized.

It was just as well, Sadie thought. It was probably better to take things a tad slower anyway. Give them both some time to make sure they were one hundred percent ready to advance their relationship before they complicated it further.

"You're going to do great," King said, taking her hand and tugging her toward him to give her a kiss on the cheek.

"How did your PR meeting go?" Sadie asked as she grabbed her handbag.

"As well as can be expected," he said with a sigh. "I've got my mom blocked for now. The last straw was when she threatened to make my life hell if I didn't send her 50K by the end of the week."

"What? Is she insane?" Sadie spat out, unable to believe that his own mother would try to extort that kind of money.

Though she guessed she shouldn't be surprised. Her father had tried to sell her mother's house without her knowledge. Some people were just monsters, and the sooner she accepted that the easier it would be for her to identify them and keep them out of her life.

"Apparently. The PR person told me to expect chaos, because people who see their family as cash cows will do whatever it takes to get some of the coin. So when—not if—she sells a story to the tabloids, then they'll set up interviews for me to set the record straight. They said that since it's documented that I was in a foster home, most of the public will believe my side and it shouldn't affect my career. I'm not looking forward to it, but it's better than being shaken down by her for the rest of my life."

Sadie gave him a hug, holding on tightly. "I'm proud of you. You deserve so much better."

He hugged her back, clinging to her as if he was trying to soak up her strength.

"I think it's time to go," she finally said as she pulled away. The nerves were back, and her stomach churned with nausea.

"Has Cosmo been out and fed?" he asked, making her heart soar that he was concerned about her dog.

"He's had dinner, but he should go out one more time."

"Okay, let's go, boy," King said, leading him to the back door.

While they were out, Sadie touched up her lipstick in the mirror near the front door and tucked a lock of hair behind her ear. "You can do this," she told herself as she did her best to bury her fears. If she just focused on King, she knew she'd get through it with flying colors.

"It's time," King said when he walked back into the room.

Cosmo had a treat in his mouth and was already cuddled up in his dog bed at the foot of the couch.

"Let's do it." She put on a brave smile and followed him out the door.

∽

"The place looks packed," King said, making Sadie's nerves dance again. He wasn't kidding. Main Street was overflowing with cars filling all the parking spaces, and there was a crowd of people milling around outside the entrance to the festival. King let out a groan.

"What is it?" Sadie asked.

"The groupies," he said, frowning.

Sadie followed his gaze and let out a small gasp. "There are so many of them."

"Yeah, it's good to have fans, but getting through them to get inside is going to be hell."

"Go around to the back. We'll park there and bypass that mess," Sadie said.

"Can we get in that way?" he asked.

"I'm sure I know someone who can get us in. Just one perk of living your whole life in a small town."

King gave her a grateful smile and circled the block before parking with a bunch of other cars that were likely vendors and people who were working the rides.

Sadie led him over to the gate that was being manned by some young kid she'd never met. "Dang it," she muttered, and then when they got close, she gave him a bright smile. "Hi there!"

"You have to go around to the front entrance." The young

SONG OF THE WITCH

man looked them over. "Not much of a costume if you ask me."

Sadie bit back a snarky reply and said, "We're supposed to go on stage in about ten minutes. Do you think you could just let us sneak by? If we have to go all the way around, we're going to be late." That much was true at least.

"Sorry." He stared down at his phone, and Sadie was ready to let him have it when she spotted an ally. Putting that smile back on her face, she called, "Deputy Reilly! You look nice this evening."

The normally surly old deputy sheriff glanced over and smiled at her as he walked toward them. "Sadie Lewis. It's been forever since I've seen you. How are you doing?"

"I'm good. Did you hear that King and I are debuting our song tonight?"

"I did. It's quite the to-do over there by the stage," the deputy said.

"That's what we heard. There's a group of fans at the entrance waiting for King who have been a little aggressive. We were hoping we could slip in the back so that we can get to the stage on time."

"I already told them that this entrance is closed," the kid said.

"It's all right, Cooper," the deputy said. "I know Sadie, and if she says there's trouble, there probably is. Let them through."

The kid looked like he wanted to argue but stepped aside anyway.

"Thank you," Sadie said and gave the deputy a quick hug. "My mom always said you were the sweetest."

The kid scoffed, and Sadie swallowed a laugh.

The deputy's face flushed pink as he said, "She was the sweet one. Have a good show, Sadie."

The deputy walked off, and the kid gaped at her. "Is that the same Deputy Sheriff Reilly that works here in Keating Hollow? Because I've never seen him bend the rules like that before."

Sadie felt a profound sense of satisfaction when she said, "He was sweet on my mother." Then she took King's hand and led him over to the tent where the stage was set up.

King chuckled. "That was smooth."

"I did my best."

Once inside, King went to find Austin while Sadie scanned the crowd from behind the makeshift bar that Keating Hollow Brewery had set up near the side door. Most everyone was dressed for Halloween, with the witch costume being the most popular. But there were plenty of vampires, werewolves, and zombies, too.

Near the back there was a press section with a few reporters and what looked like a crowd of social media influencers. Most were dressed normally, except for the influencers who'd opted to wear the looks of famous pop stars. She spotted Britney, Taylor, and Avril among the group and grinned.

And then there were, of course, King's groupies, who had somehow gotten the word he was inside and had already descended. They wore anything that showed off the most skin. Witches, maids, sexy kittens. They weren't hard to spot. Thankfully, King and Austin were in a roped off area that was being manned by security, so there was at least some barrier to keep the crowd at bay.

Sadie knew she should go in and say hello to Melissa and thank her for her wardrobe help earlier, but she just wasn't quite ready to face anyone yet. Instead, she made a beeline for the restroom just outside the tent. After using the facility and washing her hands in the mobile trailer, she stepped back outside and almost ran right into another woman.

Sadie stumbled and caught herself by grabbing the woman's arm. She quickly let go and took a step back. "Oh my gosh. I'm so sorry! Are you okay?"

"Yeah, I think so." The woman pushed her sleeve up and held her arm out, inspecting it. Then she smiled at Sadie. "No worse for the wear. Are you— Wait, are you Sadie Lewis?" There was excitement in the woman's eyes, but the longer Sadie stared at her, the more she felt an emotional coldness radiating from her. It was almost as if she was trying to force herself to be excited about meeting Sadie. Her guard automatically went up. What did this woman want from her?

"Yes, that's me," Sadie said. It wasn't as if she could lie. She'd be on stage in about ten minutes anyway. "And you are?"

"You can call me Cin. Cin with a C." The woman smiled, and her eyes lit up.

All the coldness vanished, making Sadie think she'd only imagined it, probably due to her nerves about performing. She instantly relaxed. The woman had gorgeous dark curly hair and was dressed in a stylish suit that was tailored perfectly for her runner's frame. There was no costume for this one. She was older than Sadie but obviously took care of herself, so Sadie had a hard time guessing an age. She'd say late thirties, maybe early forties. "It's nice to meet you, Cin. Do you live here in Keating Hollow, or are you just here for the show?"

"Just here for the show. Actually, I have a pretty popular TikTok channel and was invited as part of the social media outreach." She patted her chest as if looking for something and then looked down and frowned. "Oh, no. Looks like I left my press pass back at the table."

"It's all right. I believe you," Sadie said. "It's still so weird to think that I'm singing at an event that gave out press passes. I suppose the reality of all of this will eventually set in and I'll stop thinking it's all just a dream."

Cin patted her shoulder, sending a shiver of ice down Sadie's arm. She flinched slightly, causing Cin to yank her hand back. "Sorry. I didn't mean to overstep."

"You didn't. I just got a chill is all." Sadie nodded toward the tent. "I should probably get back in there."

"Wait," Cin said, shifting slightly and blocking her escape. "I was wondering since I have you here, would you mind answering a few questions for me really quick?"

"Uh, sure." Sadie was a little uncomfortable talking to the press without King or Austin there, but it probably wouldn't make a very good impression if she pushed the woman out of the way.

"Great." She pulled a tiny notebook out of her pocket and flipped it open. "You're new to the music business, correct?"

"Yep. Brand new. First song I've recorded, and it's only my second public performance," Sadie said and then wondered if she should have added the last part. If Cin went digging and found out that King had walked out on her that first night they sang together, there was no doubt she'd share that scoop. Talk about clickbait.

"It must be daunting trying to navigate it all," Cin said. "Tell me, how is it you ended up singing with King McGrath?"

"Oh, Austin Steele, our producer, put us together," she said.

"Interesting. And how did you find your producer? Did you cold call with a demo, or were there auditions? How exactly did that happen?"

These questions seemed fairly straightforward, and Sadie was starting to feel at ease answering. "That's an easy one. I work at the Keating Hollow Brewery, and Austin lives here in town. When he learned that I sing, he asked me to sing a few bars for him and… Well, the rest is history."

"So you're connected," Cin said with a nod as she jotted down some notes.

"No, I wouldn't say—"

"That's all I have for you." The woman grabbed Sadie's hand and shook it.

Sticky magic coated Sadie's hand and traveled up her forearm while the woman's intense satisfaction made Sadie's head spin. Before she could make heads or tails out of what was happening, the woman was gone, leaving Sadie with her fingers tingling as a tiny headache started to form over her right eye.

What the hell had just happened?

"Sadie?" Abby Garrison, her boss's wife, called as she poked her head out of the tent. She looked like a fairy princess with a crown of flowers on her head. "There you are. It's time. King's waiting for you."

"Right." Sadie sucked in a sharp breath, trying to clear the cobwebs in her head. Then she flexed her fingers, making sure whatever had happened with Cin hadn't affected her hand. When everything seemed normal, she pasted a smile on her face and headed into the tent to face the music.

CHAPTER 17

Sadie stood to the side of the stage next to King, barely able to hold still. The collective energy in the tent was making her feel like electricity was sparking throughout her body. The anticipation to finally perform was just as overwhelming, and it took everything in her not to bolt for the nearest exit.

King took her hand and slipped his fingers between hers, instantly calming her. He leaned into her and whispered, "You're going to be great."

"If I am, it's only because you're here." Sadie pressed her free hand to her stomach, trying to calm the butterflies.

"You'll be great because of *you*," he corrected. "And we'll kill it because we're an awesome team. Understand?"

Sadie nodded and repeated his words in her head over and over, willing herself to believe.

Austin was on the stage, thanking everyone for coming and saying something about a magical connection between the two singers as he announced their single. And the next thing Sadie knew, she heard him announce their names.

The crowd went wild, cheering and chanting their names. King squeezed her hand and said, "Showtime."

"Let's do it," Sadie heard herself say as she followed King out onto the stage. Immediately, she was bombarded with a flood of emotions. With so many bodies in the tent, there was no way to pinpoint where they came from or even their primary feelings. It was all just a jumbled mess and added a weight to her shoulders that she didn't need.

Not now. Not when she was going to pour her heart out into a song.

Concern brushed her skin in the form of tiny pinpricks. And then she heard King's voice in her mind as clear as day, *I hope she's ready for this. After tonight, she's going to be famous.*

Sadie blinked, looking around, trying to understand what just happened. She didn't hear thoughts. She was an empath, not a telepath. Had she imagined that? But there was no time to worry about it. The band had already started playing the intro of the song.

Briggs appeared out of nowhere and handed her guitar to her. The moment the instrument was in her hands, her nerves settled and her mind quieted. Sadie let out a huge sigh of relief.

King gave her a look, asking if she was ready. She nodded once and started to strum her guitar. He grinned and together they threw themselves into their song.

Summer nights, they were yours
Moonlit streams, I saw magic, you saw me
You shared your secrets, I swear, they're still safe after the storms

Sadie stared into King's eyes as she gave everything she had to the song that meant so much to her. It was their song. Their story. And every time she sang it now, she was filled with love and hope and promise. And so was he. She could feel him in her bones.

The audience faded away. All she saw was the man standing beside her, singing with his angelic voice. He'd drawn her in, and love was bursting from him, engulfing her, making her feel powerful and loved and invincible.

Singing with him was just *incredible.*

Sadie was so lost in the song, so lost in King that she barely noticed when magic started to crawl over her. It was faint at first, just a tingle here and there, but then Sadie started to pulse with it as if she were maybe feeding off the audience instead of the other way around.

And when the song ended, Sadie and King stared at each other for far too long, right up until the magic that had been surrounding her suddenly vanished.

Sadie felt cold and exposed, and all she wanted to do was run out of there. But they had another song to sing. King's song. She turned to look at the musicians behind her, wondering why they hadn't started to play, and she was startled when the woman who played keyboard suddenly stood and said, "You're an asshole." She flipped her bandmate off and stormed off the stage.

"What the hell?" Sadie turned back to King, finding a pained expression on his face. "What's happening?"

"Come on." He grabbed her hand and hauled her off the stage.

"But we're supposed to do another song," she said, flustered and confused as the crowd noise raised from a dull roar to almost unbearable levels.

"Look, Sadie," he said as he waved to the crowd. "Something's wrong. Can't you feel it?"

They were standing behind the temporary bar, looking

out at the crowd. She noted that a lot of them seemed to be arguing, but Sadie couldn't *feel* their emotions. She jerked, startled by the realization. Anger was an intense feeling, and when she was around someone, anyone really, who was upset, she could feel it all the way down to her bones.

But now? It felt as if her emotional detector was broken. There was just a void. All she felt was an eerie silence. It unnerved her.

What was happening?

"I've got to get out of here," King said, cringing and backing away. He tugged at her hand, but Sadie was rooted to the ground, still trying to make sense of her new reality. He shook his head as his hand slipped out of hers. "It's too much. I can't take it."

"King?" she called as he disappeared out of the tent.

"Why are you being so selfish?" a familiar voice cried right in front of Sadie. She spun and found Candy screaming at Hanna. They were both dressed up as bakers and had cupcake fascinators on their heads. "You knew I had plans, and you went ahead and put me down to close anyway. It's always all about you!"

Hanna exploded on her cousin, yelling something about the scheduling and how if Candy wanted more responsibility she needed to step up.

"Hey!" Sadie said, stepping up to them. "Ladies, please. Let's take a step back and—"

"Stay out of it!" they both shouted at the same time.

Sadie put her hands up and backed away, moving down the bar to find Melissa in a Spice Girls costume, standing with Briggs, who hadn't bothered to dress up.

"Why didn't you take me home the other night, Briggs?"

Melissa ran her finger down his chest. "I know you wanted me."

Lust burned in Brigg's gaze before he dipped his head and kissed her so fiercely that Sadie thought they might just go up in flames.

"Melissa!" a man called, his tone sharp. "What are you doing?"

Sadie gasped when she saw Jasper in a caveman costume making a beeline for Briggs and Melissa.

"Jasper? What are you doing here? And why are you wearing that? You look ridiculous." Melissa eyed him, looking confused. "I thought after that disastrous concert I'd never see you again."

"I texted you and told you I forgive you," he said, sounding like a petulant child. "I told you I'd be here, and now I find you with this guy? Haven't you hurt me enough?"

Melissa blinked at him. "Hurt you? I barely know you. And you're the creep who tried to manhandle me. This is going nowhere."

"Stop!" Jasper shook his head violently and then looked at the man behind him. He was tall, dressed up in a suit and cape as a rich vampire, and he was staring at Jasper, his beautiful eyes filled with frustration. Jasper let out an irritated groan and then said, "How am I going to keep convincing everyone I'm not in love with Brandon if I can't keep a girlfriend?"

"What?" Melissa asked as she looked between the two men.

Jasper clasped his hand over his mouth and then pushed passed everyone, heading for the door. The man Sadie assumed was Brandon ran after him. "Jas, wait!"

All around her, people were arguing. Everyone except

Shannon and Brian Knox. Shannon was Silas Ansell's sister. She managed his career and was a good friend of the Townsends. Shannon was dressed as a sexy nurse and was pressed up against her husband, Brian, her leg wrapped around his waist as she ran her thumb over his lips. His hands were gripping her ass, and Sadie expected them to rip each other's clothes off at any moment.

Instead, Shannon glanced around and then looked right at her husband and said, "I'm so horny you better take me home right now, or I'm going to have my way with you in the bathroom."

Brian grabbed her hand and started to pull her toward the side door that led to the bathrooms.

Sadie jumped in front of them and pointed to the exit. "Not here, guys. Trust me, you don't want to do that in a public restroom. Head on home."

Shannon groaned and then giggled as she said, "There's always the back seat."

Brian spun abruptly, and the two pushed their way outside.

Sadie just hoped they didn't make a spectacle of themselves before they found somewhere private.

When the chaos extended to Abby and Clay as they argued about who should announce that the bar was closing, Sadie took it upon herself to end the madness. She got back up on stage, grabbed the microphone, and said, "Ladies and gentlemen, thank you for coming tonight, but it's time to pack it in. The festival is closing. Please grab your things and —" Before Sadie could even finish, the patrons all made a beeline for the exit. The pushing and name calling started almost immediately. Sadie frowned and added, "Please leave

SONG OF THE WITCH

in an orderly fashion and be kind to everyone else trying to make it home tonight."

Her words seemed to help as the crowd suddenly began to mellow and started exiting without trying to run each other over.

King was suddenly at her side as she stepped off the stage and exited the side door of the tent. "How did you do that?"

"I don't know," she said, still confused. "It's like everyone is possessed."

He nodded, staring at her with worry in his eyes, but she couldn't feel anything radiating off him like she normally would.

"Are you doing okay?" Sadie asked him, looking for any signs of possession or agitation or anything that resembled the crowd's over-the-top reactions.

"Yeah. I was just overwhelmed by the intensity of people's thoughts. I've always gotten snippets, but nothing like that."

Sadie had known that King had telepathic abilities. Just as he'd always known she was an empath. Neither had been bothered by the other's abilities since they both understood what a burden it was to be subjected to other people's thoughts and emotions. She grabbed his hand and squeezed.

He squeezed back and said, "We'd better find Austin."

They started to head toward the back entrance, but when they reached the tent's exit, King paused, squinting in the darkness. "That's not—no way. It can't be."

"What?" Sadie followed his gaze and caught a glimpse of the woman who'd cornered her outside the bathrooms earlier before they'd taken the stage.

"That was my mother." King took off at a run, leaving Sadie alone and shellshocked.

CHAPTER 18

*K*ing broke out into a sprint, zigzagging through the departing attendees, and he was out of breath when he finally made it to the entrance of the festival. His heart was pounding while fury flowed through his veins. He'd never imagined that his mother would show up in Keating Hollow or at the festival. But more importantly, why? To confront him directly? If so, then why hadn't she done so already? Had she just arrived before the show?

He glanced around the parking lot but didn't see anyone who looked like his mother. Frustrated, he walked back in, intending to go find Sadie, but stopped in his tracks when he spotted a group of his dedicated fans. He had to find a way to get around them before they noticed him. King took a couple of steps back, thinking he'd go the long way around back to the tent, but then he heard one of them squeal, "It's King! He's right there."

He spun and ran out the entrance then took a sharp right into a residential area. When he was sure the groupies weren't following him anymore, he took out his phone and texted Sadie. *On my way back there. Meet me at the Jeep.*

It took King almost a half hour to walk all the way back to where his car was parked, and he was relieved to find Sadie standing next to his Jeep, staring at her phone. She looked up, startled as if she hadn't heard him. "There you are. Did you find her?"

Shaking his head, he walked over and kissed her temple. "Come on. I'm more than ready to be home."

"Same." Once they were both in, he slammed the Jeep into reverse and sped out of there just as the group of fans showed up, their camera phones raised as they filmed him leaving.

"My goddess, don't they ever give up?" Sadie said and turned around in her seat, staring at them.

"Unfortunately, no. Do you think there's some sort of spell we can get that's a fan repellent?" he asked.

Sadie snorted her amusement. "I'd buy a case." Then she sobered. "I hate that they make it so difficult for you."

"Yeah. It's not the pleasant side of this industry. Usually it's not this bad, but this group seems to be determined."

"Maybe you can talk to Drew and see if there's something that can be done. Harassment charges or something," she said.

He nodded, but his mind had already moved on from the groupies. He couldn't stop thinking about what his mother was going to do next.

"Are you sure that was your mother?" Sadie asked.

"I'm positive," he said definitively.

Sadie was silent until they pulled into the driveway of Brigg's house. As King pulled in next to Brigg's SUV, she said, "I spoke to your mother before the show."

SONG OF THE WITCH

"What?" King asked as he slammed on the brakes, making the Jeep jerk to a stop. "Why? When? What did she say?"

"I didn't know it was her. She told me her name was Cin and that she had a press pass because she has a popular TikTok account for music."

"Her name is Cindy, so that tracks," he said bitterly. "But a TikTok channel?" He snorted. "That has to be a lie. If she did, she'd certainly use me for clout, and I'd have heard about it by now." He narrowed his eyes at Sadie. "What did she want?"

"She asked me how I was discovered and how I ended up singing with you. I just told her that I knew Austin and he put us together. That's it."

King ran his hands through his hair and let out a frustrated growl. Then without a word, he got out of the Jeep and headed up to the house.

Sadie hurried after him. "I'm sorry, King. I had no idea who she was, or I would have warned you."

"I know," he said. "You don't need to apologize." He was so in his head that he didn't even notice the envelope taped to the front door until Sadie said, "There's a letter for you."

"What?"

She pointed to the door. "Look."

Right there in front of him was an envelope with the name *Kevin* scrawled across the front. There was no mistaking the handwriting. It was his mother's. She'd been there, so not only was she at the show, but she now knew where he was living.

"Dammit!" He ripped the envelope off the door and stomped in.

Briggs was sitting on the couch in his sweats, eating straight out of an ice cream container, looking like he was coming down from a bender. His hair was wet, indicating he'd taken a shower, but his eyes were bloodshot, and he looked like he hadn't slept in a week.

"What happened to you?" King asked as he studied the letter in his hands.

"No idea," Briggs said. "One minute I was fine, ready to spend the night in bed with a hottie, and the next I felt like I'd had the crap kicked out of me. So keep your distance. I probably have a bug or something."

"Was that hottie Melissa?" Sadie asked, her tone amused.

"As a matter of fact, it was. But then she wasn't feeling so hot either, so I dropped her off at the inn where she's staying until her plumbing is finished, and then I came home."

"She's staying at the inn?" Sadie asked. "I thought her house was supposed to be done already." She pulled out her phone and started tapping on the screen while Cosmo pawed at her leg. Glancing down at her dog, she said, "Come on, Cosmo. I'll take you out while we call Auntie Melissa."

Once Sadie was gone, King sank into a chair and studied the outside of the envelope. Then he looked up. "Was this on the door when you got here?"

Briggs squinted at the envelope. "No. I don't think so."

"How long have you been here?"

"I dunno. Fifteen minutes? Long enough to take a quick shower, change into sweats, and find my Toffee Almond Swirl."

"She must have taped it on the door when you were showering," King said.

"Who did?"

"My mother."

Brigg's eyes widened. "Cindy was here?"

King made a disgusted face as he nodded. "I saw her in

the parking lot behind the tent after the show. And Sadie said she cornered her earlier, though she didn't know the woman she was talking to was my mother."

"And she left that letter on the door." Briggs shook his head. "Are you going to open it?"

"Yeah." King stared down at the envelope and then suddenly ripped it open. He scanned it and swore. Loudly.

Kevin,

I know you're upset. You've proven your point. But you can't keep ignoring your mother. Send the money you promised, and I'll make sure your girlfriend recovers from her unfortunate malady.

Mom.

"What does it say?" Briggs asked.

King handed him the letter and then fell back into the chair, staring at the ceiling, his insides boiling with pure rage. What had she done? King racked his brain for possibilities, desperately hoping that the letter was only a bluff. But in his heart, he knew it wasn't. He'd felt the magical power consuming him and Sadie when they'd been on that stage and could no longer deny the truth that was staring him in the face.

"What does this mean?" Briggs asked.

King shifted his gaze to his best friend and said, "I'm pretty sure my mother cursed Sadie."

CHAPTER 19

"Melissa?" Sadie said into the phone.

"Yeah, I'm here." Her friend sounded out of sorts and not at all like herself.

Sadie sat in the wicker chair on the back porch as she watched Cosmo sniff around the small patch of grass. "Are you all right? What's wrong?"

"I think I ate something bad. I don't know. I'm nauseous and I've got the beginning of a headache. I'm just going to drink some ginger ale and go to bed."

"I'm sure that's a good idea. Briggs isn't feeling all that great either. Maybe it's a bug going around."

"Maybe," Melissa said.

"Do you need me to get you anything? Ginger ale? Pain medication? Something to settle your stomach?"

"Yeah, okay," she said, sounding pathetic.

"I'm on my way. Text if you think of anything else you need." Sadie ended the call, and when Cosmo was done, she went back inside and grabbed her keys. "I've got to run out and get some stuff for Melissa. She's feeling even worse than you, Briggs." She looked at the man still holding his ice cream container. "Do you need anything?"

He shook his head, his expression grim. "I'll be okay. Tell Mel I'm sorry. She probably got this bug from me."

"You both got sick at the same time. I'm guessing it was someone else at the festival. Don't worry about it. I'm sure she doesn't blame you. I'll be back in a bit." She started to head toward the door, but when she saw the dark expression on King's face, she paused. "What is it?" She turned to King. "It's the letter, isn't it? What did your mother say?"

King shook his head. "Just more bullshit. Don't worry about it. Go take care of your friend. I'll be here when you get back."

Sadie wanted to protest but recognized that maybe King needed some time to process. So she walked over and gave him a kiss on the head and called to Cosmo. "Let's go, buddy. Auntie Mel is gonna need some snuggles."

Twenty minutes later, Sadie knocked on Melissa's door at the Keating Hollow Inn.

"It's open," Melissa called.

Sadie walked in with a bag in one hand and Cosmo's leash in the other. She found Melissa buried in the covers of the bed, her clothes strewn all over the room. "Hey."

"Hey," Melissa said without moving.

"I brought reinforcements." She put the bag on Melissa's nightstand and unhooked Cosmo's leash. "Cosmo wants to make sure you're okay."

Melissa poked her head out from under the covers and gave the dog a weak smile. "Hey boy. Come here."

Sadie set him down right next to her friend and was silent as she petted him. When Melissa finally stopped, he leaned into her side, snuggling the way he always did.

Melissa smiled at him. "He's a good dog."

"He is." Sadie handed her a ginger ale. "How are you doing?"

"Awful." She pushed herself up, letting the covers fall.

Sadie's eyes widened as she noticed the T-shirt her friend was wearing. The graphic was a picture of her and King with moonlight shining down on them. Below the photo, it had the lyric, *I see you in my dreams, reflected in the midnight streams.* "Where did you get that?"

Melissa frowned at her. "At the festival. Where else?"

"I had no idea we had merch already," Sadie said, shaking her head.

"They were in the gift bags." Melissa took a sip of the ginger ale and grimaced.

"Not the right kind?"

"It is, I just…" Melissa shook her head. "Whatever this is, it's kicking my ass." She curled up again, hugging a pillow.

Sadie laid down on the bed next to her with Cosmo between them, intending to be quiet and let her friend rest, but instead, Melissa said, "I won't be back into my house until next week."

"What?" Sadie gasped out. "Why? I thought it was only going to take a few days?"

She made a small, irritated noise. "That's what they said at first, but now they're saying they're waiting for some valve for the septic and that there are more pipes that need to be replaced. I don't know. It just means I'm stuck here for a while longer."

"I'm sorry, hun. I'm sure that's gotta be rough on the budget. Maybe you can come and stay in my room at Brigg's place."

"Hell no," she said into the pillow. "That's not happening."

Sadie stared down at her, noting the scowl on Melissa's face. "I thought you two liked each other. Didn't I see you kissing at the show?"

"Screw him. The man is the worst kind around. Acting like he likes me, being sweet and protective, buying me drinks and being attentive. Not to mention the searing hot kiss he laid on me. But when I asked him out, I've never seen a man run so fast. It's like he's allergic to anything that isn't a one-night stand. You couldn't pay me to stay in his house."

Hadn't King said his friend wasn't much for commitment? He'd said he was a shameless flirt who never really got serious about anyone. "If it helps, I don't think it's you. King mentioned that he doesn't really date."

"Well then, he should stop being so wonderful!" Melissa cried and then squeezed her eyes shut. "Goddess, I sound pathetic. Don't listen to me. I'm just feeling sorry for myself after everything that's happened this week. First the fiasco with Jasper and then my plumbing goes bad, which is costing me a fortune by the way, and then I get rejected by the guy I really like. Do you know how long it's been since I've gone out with someone who makes my stomach flutter instead of just settling for someone and hoping they work out?"

"Ages?" Sadie offered.

"You can say that again. I think the last time I dated someone I really enjoyed being around was when we were in high school. Remember Dare Deckman?"

Sadie nodded and then said, "Didn't he turn out to be gay? Or at least bi? I think I heard he married a man."

"Ugh! Of course he is." Melissa shook her head. "That explains Jasper, I guess. I seem to attract men who really aren't all that interested in me."

"That's because you're so open and they trust you," Sadie

said, wrapping an arm around her shoulders. "Dare really cared about you. I think if he was straight and you two met now, you'd have a real chance."

"Not helping," Melissa said dryly. "Besides, that doesn't explain Jasper using me as a beard or Briggs acting like he's interested and then running the moment I return that interest."

"Sorry." Sadie let out a soft chuckle. "Jasper… He's a head case who needs to find a way to live his authentic self. As for Briggs, I don't know his story, but it's not a reflection on you. Trust me. I know you better than anyone else, and if I was a man, I'd date you."

"You would not." Melissa laughed, sounding better than she had since Sadie walked into the room. "I'm way too social for you."

"That's what I like about you." Sadie winked at her. "You keep me from being a hermit."

"You can't fool me," she said. "But thanks for trying to cheer me up."

Cosmo lifted his head and gave her a kiss on her cheek.

She laughed. "Thank you, too, little one." Melissa sighed and took another sip of the ginger ale. This time it appeared to go down easier. "I think you two saved me. The nausea is fading, and my head feels better."

"Want me to order food?" Sadie asked.

Melissa pressed a hand to her stomach and shook her head. "That might be a bridge too far. I think I'll just sleep it off. Thanks for coming by. You helped."

Sadie slipped off the bed and put Cosmo on the floor. "You know I'd do anything for you. Get some rest. There are painkillers in the bag along with crackers if you need something to settle your stomach."

Melissa thanked her again before Sadie and Cosmo headed back to Brigg's place.

On the way, she thought about Briggs, wondering what kept him from getting serious about anyone. Because in her mind, he and Melissa were perfect for each other. Briggs was steady and fun, and so was Melissa. They were the type of people everyone loved because they were always up for something fun, but at the end of the day, they were there to take care of the people they loved.

They were the people that she and King were lucky to have.

When she got back to the house, the porch light was on, but both King and Briggs had gone to bed.

"Looks like we need to lock up," Sadie said to Cosmo.

Once the place was buttoned up, Sadie retreated to her room, got ready for bed, and then laid there with Cosmo by her side, staring at the ceiling. It was killing her that King's awful mother had come to town and she had no idea how to help him. Finally, she threw the covers back and crept down the hall to his room.

She knocked softly. "King?"

Footsteps sounded on the hardwood just before the door opened. He wore nothing but low-slung pajama pants. Her eyes drifted over his torso, taking in his six-pack abs and muscular pecs.

"Whoa," she said softly.

His lips curved into a sexy half smile as he pulled her into the room.

"I came to see how you're doing," she said.

"Better now." King pressed his palms to her cheeks and leaned in, kissing her so thoroughly that by the time he pulled back she was breathless.

"Okay. That was nice, but—"

King put his forefinger to her lips and whispered, "Do you really want to talk right now?"

Sadie shook her head. She really didn't. After all the years of dreaming of King and him coming back into her life, all she wanted was him. She wanted to finally understand what it meant to be his. "No talking," she said and led him over to the bed.

He ran his hands down her arms and then slipped his hands underneath her pajama top and held them there at her waist, his fingers caressing her bare skin. "Are you sure about this? If we take this step, you're mine, Sadie Lewis, do you understand that?"

"I'm sure." She knew what she wanted. And that was King McGrath.

"Finally," he murmured as he glided his lips over her neck and stripped her shirt off, leaving her just as bare as he was. "Gods, you're magnificent," he said as he pulled her down onto the bed, where the entire world slipped away as they got lost in each other.

CHAPTER 20

King woke with a smile on his face. The night before had been nothing short of magical. He'd known it would be special if he ever spent the night with Sadie, but he hadn't realized that he'd be a total goner. The love that had radiated between them filled his soul, made him whole, and he knew without a shadow of a doubt that he wanted to spend the rest of his life with her.

He reached for her, but when his hand only found an empty bed, he opened his eyes and glanced around. She was gone, but there was a note on her pillow.

King,

You were sound asleep and looked so peaceful that I didn't want to wake you. I had to go to work. If you have time, come by if you can. Thank you for last night. It was wonderful.

Love, Sadie.

"Damn," he muttered, already missing holding her. He threw the covers back and stumbled out into the hallway bathroom.

Thirty minutes later, when he was showered and dressed,

he walked into the kitchen to find Briggs sitting at the table. He was kicked back, drinking a cup of coffee as he read something on his laptop. There was a stack of waffles along with fresh strawberries and whipped cream in the middle of the table.

"Wow, nice spread," King said. "Did you do all this?"

Briggs nodded and grinned at him. "I figured you'd need a good breakfast to replenish all those calories after last night."

King raised one eyebrow, but otherwise didn't respond. He wasn't surprised that his friend was needling him about his night with Sadie. But King wasn't taking the bait. His time with Sadie wasn't up for discussion. What they shared was between them and them alone.

"Oh, it's like that, is it?" Briggs said, looking serious. Then he nodded. "Yeah, I figured that was how that'd go."

"You did?" King asked as he got himself a cup of coffee.

"Anyone with eyes could see you'd fallen hard for that girl. Good for you, man. I'm happy for you both."

"Thanks." King sat at the table and helped himself to a waffle. He doctored it with the strawberries and whipped cream. "You must be feeling better to get up and make all this."

"I am. Whatever that was last night, it's gone now. In fact, I feel great. And so should you. Look at this." He turned his computer around so that King could see the article from one of the most respected music critics in the game. The headline read, *Look out, world. There's a new duo in town, and you're going to fall in love just like I did.*

King scanned the article and then scanned it again. It was two full pages of how much the author loved the new single. He broke down all the elements of the song and ended by saying he'd be the first one in line for the concert tickets.

"And look at this." He pulled up his music streaming service. Right there on the Hot 100 new releases was King and Sadie's song. "It's trending everywhere. Streaming stations and social media sites. King, my bro, you and Sadie have a hit on your hands."

King sat back in his chair, stunned. He'd known the song was good. Felt it was great even. But he hadn't expected this. Not this fast. Usually it took time for songs to build. But this felt like... magic.

There was that word again. King decided that Sadie was the reason. *She* was magic, and as far as he was concerned, everything she touched became magical.

But then suddenly a dark cloud formed over him as he remembered the note his mother had left the night before and how he'd been so convinced Sadie had been cursed. Had he imagined that? Last night, when she'd come back from seeing Melissa, she'd seemed completely normal. There hadn't been a sign of any sort of a curse.

Had his mother been messing with him? He wouldn't have put it past her. But then what had happened when they were on stage last night? King had never felt that sort of magical energy when they'd sung previously. Sure, he'd heard her thoughts, and he was certain she'd felt his emotions, but it hadn't been all consuming like that with magic sparking everywhere. It had almost been like he and Sadie were sucking all the emotional energy out of the room, and then when they were done singing everyone had gone apeshit.

He just didn't know what it meant, and it frustrated him. He had to talk to Sadie. That's all there was to it. King glanced at the clock. She'd likely have her break in a few hours. He'd go down to the brewery then and tell her about the note.

King turned to Briggs. "Can I ask you something?"

"Like what? Do you have questions about the birds and the bees? It sounded like you knew what you were doing, but I suppose those moans could have been from disappointment," Briggs said with a cocky grin.

"Shut it. It's not about that, and nobody was disappointed in anything."

Briggs snickered. "If you say so."

King rolled his eyes. His friend could be so juvenile sometimes. "Why do you never get serious with anyone?"

"Uh, what?" Briggs asked, looking taken aback. "What kind of question is that? Are you trying to marry me off to someone?"

"No." King shook his head. "Not at all. You can stay single for the rest of your life if that's what makes you happy. Or get married and pop out a few kids." King glanced around the kitchen. "Just leave a room for me, will you?"

"There's always a room for you, dumbass. You're family." Briggs shifted his gaze away and added, "My only family."

"Exactly," King said. "We're the only family we have, you and me. And I have to be honest; I'm hoping that Sadie and I can make a life together, too."

"Is this you telling me that I'm being replaced or something?" Briggs asked with a forced laugh.

King sat back and stared at his friend. "Are you serious right now? Do you really think that there is anyone who could replace you? That I'd drop you because I found Sadie?"

"Well, no. But that's what it sounds like you're saying." He got up abruptly and took his plate to the sink. "No matter what happens, if you marry Sadie or someone else, you have a place with me and so will she. I don't even know why we're having this conversation." He rinsed his plate and shoved it in the dishwasher.

"Because you deserve more, Briggs," King said softly. "More than just me."

His friend didn't turn around to look at him when he said, "Let it go, King. I'm fine. I don't need a woman to make me happy." Then he left the kitchen, his head bowed.

King let out a long sigh, wondering how he'd messed that up so badly. All he'd wanted to do was… Hell, he didn't even know exactly what he was trying to do. Briggs was a grown man. He could navigate his own love life any way he pleased.

It was just that deep down, King thought he knew Briggs well enough to know that he *did* need someone. Someone more than just King. Someone he could devote himself to. He was a caregiver. He was always doing things like making them breakfast and protecting King from fans. He had a lot of love to give. There was no doubt about it.

King also knew that despite Briggs's brash joking about womanizing and only wanting one-night stands, the truth was, he rarely hooked up with anyone who wasn't a friends-with-benefits situation. And since Briggs had moved to Keating Hollow, King didn't think he'd even had one of those. He just wanted more for his friend. Whatever that looked like.

After King cleaned up the kitchen, he took Cosmo on a walk and then jumped into his Jeep and headed to the studio.

"King!" Austin said when King walked into his office. "How's my favorite pop star this morning?"

"I'm good. How are things going here?" He sat in the chair across from Austin.

"Fantastic. Listen, I'm glad you stopped by." Austin tapped

on a legal pad he had on his desk and asked, "Do you know what this is?"

"Paper?" King said, just to be a smartass.

Austin ignored him. "It's a list of media outlets that either want a live performance or an interview with both you and Sadie. The phone has been ringing off the hook this morning. That performance last night... I'm telling you, King, it was pure magic. Everyone is talking about it. I've never seen anything take off this fast before. We've got to get you and Sadie out on the road as soon as possible. Capitalizing on this is going to make your single the song of the year. Mark my words."

"Hey, that's great," King said, trying to quiet the voice in his head that was warning him that his mother had done something to Sadie. He just didn't know what yet. And committing to a grueling marketing blitz before they figured it out didn't seem like a great idea. "Listen, Austin, has my mother popped up in the news yet?"

"Nope. But I'd be prepared for it now," he said, suddenly serious. "Once she sees all these headlines, she's going to be right back at your door asking for another handout."

"I figured," he said, feeling defeated. He knew she was in town, and he'd be on edge until she made her next move.

"I'm sorry, man. I've never been in your shoes, but I do know what it feels like when your family isn't who you want them to be." Austin leaned back in his chair and then suddenly let out an amused huff. "Of course, I found out my father was shitty because he was possessed by a ghost, but that's probably not your mother's issue." He paused and raised both eyebrows. "Though it wouldn't hurt to check."

"I should only be so lucky," King muttered. "But she's always been shit, so not likely."

"You never know. That ghost took up residence in my father for a decade."

"Huh." King wished with all his heart that he could blame his mother's behavior on a possession, but somehow, he just knew that wasn't in the cards for him. "You know, if the opportunity comes up, I might look into that just to rule it out."

"Couldn't hurt," Austin said. "In the meantime, stick to the plan that PR came up with. The last thing you want to do is let your mother take what isn't hers. We'll be behind you every step of the way. Don't worry about that. Plus with how big this song is going to be and your already solid fan base, nothing is going to stop you now. Enjoy it, okay?"

"Sure, boss." King stood. "Thanks for the pep talk."

"Anytime," Austin said. "And King?"

"Yeah?"

"Congratulations."

CHAPTER 21

Sadie was busy wiping down the counter when Clay and Abby walked in together. "Hey! How's it going?" she asked them. "I hope you guys weren't out too late, breaking down the bar after we debuted our song."

"Oh, we were there late all right," Abby said, taking a seat at the bar. "Then when we got home, both of us were sicker than a dog."

"Oh, no! Melissa and Briggs weren't feeling well either," Sadie said. "Why are you here? You should be in bed recovering."

"Oh, no." Abby smiled brightly. "We woke up just fine. Must have been something we ate."

"Abby forced one of her potions down my throat last night," Clay said, getting himself a glass of water. "I have to admit, even though it tasted like dirt, it seemed to do the trick."

"It did not taste like dirt," Abby insisted. "It tastes like grass. The main ingredient is wheatgrass."

"Yeah, it tastes like grass and dirt," he said. "I'm not

complaining, though. It worked, so as far as I'm concerned, you're the hero in this scenario."

Abby beamed at him. "This is why I married him."

Sadie chuckled. "Good call."

"Can you get me a cheeseburger, cheese fries, and a slice of apple pie? And coffee. Definitely coffee," Abby added. "I'm starving today."

"Goodness, I guess you are feeling better." Sadie put her order in and got to work making a fresh pot of coffee.

When she brought the fresh pot back, she was pleased to see Melissa and Imogen sitting next to Abby. "Hey! I didn't know you two were coming in today."

"I needed to get the scoop on everything that went down last night," Imogen said. "I can't believe I missed it! The party I coordinated went overtime, and I had to track down someone at the party store to even get the tables and chairs back, and it was just a nightmare. Being that it was Halloween, no one wanted to come in. They only did it because I promised to recommend them to future clients. Otherwise, I'd be on the road right now taking them back to Eureka."

"I'm glad you're here, instead," Sadie said. "Let me get your orders in and then we can chat." After she sent the orders to the kitchen, Sadie poured some drinks and went back to her friend. "Okay, I'm back. Where were we?"

"I was saying I'm sorry I missed your performance." Imogen reached across the bar and squeezed Sadie's hand. "I heard it was spectacular."

"It was something all right," Melissa said, making Abby chuckle.

"What does that mean?" Imogen asked. "Did something happen? Don't tell me something spooky happened with it being Halloween and all. You do know that's a day when the spirits come lurking, right? Especially here in Keating Hollow."

"You've been listening to your sister too long," Melissa said flippantly. Then suddenly she winced, turned to Imogen, and added, "I didn't mean that. I wasn't thinking."

"It's all right," Imogen said, her voice tight.

It wasn't that long ago when Imogen had been possessed by a ghost. An evil one that had made her life hell. Her sister Harlow was a famous ghost hunter, and even she hadn't realized it. The entire situation had been very traumatic.

"It's not all right. I'm sorry I was so thoughtless," Melissa said.

"Thank you, but really, that's in the past. Don't worry about it." Imogen turned to Sadie. "Did it go okay? I saw that your song is trending on TikTok."

"It is?" Sadie lit up. "That's amazing! It's probably because the PR firm invited influencers." The image of King's mother flashed in her mind, and she quickly squashed it. King had said there was no way she was an influencer, so if the song was doing well, it wasn't because she had anything to do with it.

"Sounds like you have a decent PR team," Abby said. "That's fantastic."

"So, if the song is doing well, then what was it?" Imogen asked again. "Something went down at the show last night. I can feel it."

"Order up!" the cook called from the order window.

"Excuse me," Sadie said and went to get Abby's lunch. "Here you go. One cheeseburger, a side of cheese fries, and the best apple pie this side of the Mississippi."

"Good goddess, that looks delicious," Abby said as she

plucked a cheesy fry off the plate and shoved the entire thing into her mouth. Moaning with pleasure, she nodded her approval and dug into the greasy goodness.

Sadie went back to stand in front of Imogen. "Last night was pretty crazy. Honestly, the song went better than expected. King and I were both in the zone and everything was perfect. I felt better than ever, and the crowd seemed to be into it. It was only after we finished our song that all hell broke loose."

"What do you mean? Was there a fire or a medical emergency or something of that nature?" Imogen asked.

"Nope. None of those things," Sadie replied. "King and I sang the song and then afterward, everyone seemed to sort of lose their minds."

"How?" Imogen frowned. "Over-the-top cheering? Cause I gotta say, that sounds like a good thing."

"No," Melissa said. "Well, there was a lot of cheering, but that's not what Sadie means."

Abby let out a choked laugh. "Yeah, after the song was over, Clay and I got into a huge fight over who was going to make the announcement that everyone had to leave. And I do mean huge. Which is weird because we never fight about that kind of thing."

Imogen studied her, seeming unimpressed.

Sadie supposed a couple fighting about something so mundane probably didn't hit anyone's radar as strange, but she'd been around Clay and Abby since the beginning, and it was true; they rarely fought about anything. And when they did, it was about things much more important than making an announcement.

"I also made out with Briggs," Melissa said as she pointed to the beer taps.

"Where?" Imogen asked, her eyes wide.

"Right there in the tent in front of god and everyone," Melissa said. "Usually I'm a lot more modest."

"When?" Imogen joked.

"Ha. Ha." Melissa said dryly. "I just felt like something came over me—"

"Yeah, lust," Abby said with a snicker.

"Besides that." Melissa shook her head. "It was like all my filters were just gone, and I couldn't stop myself even though I knew I'd regret it."

"You regret kissing Briggs?" Sadie asked her, feeling a little sorry for her friend.

"No, I mean yes… Well, sort of?" Melissa blew out a breath and made a face. "I mean, it's not like I regret the actual kiss. He's a great kisser. It was the way it happened and where it happened. I suppose I'm just a romantic, but I'd have preferred something more special than in the middle of a rowdy crowd or with that confused jackass Jasper adding his two cents."

"That makes sense," Sadie said with a nod. She wouldn't have liked her first kiss with King to be in that scenario either.

"The crowd was beyond rowdy. More like out of control," Abby said.

Imogen leaned forward to look past Melissa so she could see Abby. "How so?"

"Well, there were a lot of couples arguing. And then there were Shannon and Brian, who I swear were about to rip their clothes off right then and there until Sadie redirected them. I mean, I know they are hot for each other pretty much *all* the time, but they are never that in people's faces about it."

"Hmm, it kind of sounds like everyone was possessed," Imogen said. "Except for the fact that you all were there, and I can't see any signs that you're carrying a crazy spirit with you. And I'd know since... Well, it happened to me."

"I definitely don't think I have a passenger on board," Abby said. "If I did, I vomited him or her out when I was emptying my guts last night before I finally thought to suck down a potion."

"You were sick last night, too?" Melissa asked, pushing her dark hair out of her eyes.

"Yes. Both Clay and I were super nauseous. I was the one who ended up losing my dinner. He almost did though. But after we took the potions, we started to get better right away and then woke up just fine this morning." She waved at her food. "As you can see, I'm not having issues keeping anything down today."

"Me either, and I didn't even take a potion," Melissa said. "Though my bestie did come through with some much-needed ginger ale and crackers."

Sadie caught her eye and smiled at her.

"You mean I didn't have to drink the dirt potion?" Clay called out from his spot at the other end of the bar.

"I'm sure it helped," Melissa called back as she gave Abby an apologetic grimace.

Abby waved it off. "He'll thank me when he adds ten to twenty years to his life because of me."

"True," Clay called again, and everyone laughed.

But then Imogen sobered. "You know, as someone who is hearing about the situation last night, it does sound like something strange went down. It's unusual for everyone's collective energy to change so suddenly. Are you sure someone didn't cast a spell over everyone?"

A shiver ran down Sadie's spine. She hadn't thought about it that closely, but the way that Imogen described it was spot on. There *had* been an overall energy change. And it happened after Sadie had been reveling in all the magic she and King had been creating.

Then it hit her like a bolt of lightning.

The collective energy in the room had magically changed right after Sadie, an empath, had created a seriously intense magic with King.

"I think it was me," Sadie said, her voice small and full of fear. "I'm the one who cursed everyone."

CHAPTER 22

"What? That's crazy," Melissa said dismissively. "You can't curse anyone. You don't even have any magic."

"I don't…" Sadie shook her head and backed away from the bar as if she was going to bolt.

King had just walked into the brewery and heard Sadie say she thought she was the one who'd cursed everyone the night before. And as crazy as it sounded, he thought that she might be right.

"Sadie!" he called as he hurried over to her.

She stood behind the bar, blinking at him like a deer in the headlights. "I think I'd better go… I don't know, somewhere besides here."

"Oh no, you don't." King slipped behind the counter and wrapped an arm around her waist, giving her the support she so clearly needed.

"But I have to. I have to figure out what I did. See a healer or something," she said, searching his gaze.

"Hold on." He looked at the women sitting at the bar and

said, "Excuse us for a minute." Then he took her by the hand and led her to the hallway that accessed the restrooms just to give them some privacy. "Now, tell me what's going on."

She swallowed, looking a little shaken. "We were talking about what happened last night, telling Imogen about it. When we told her how everyone was acting afterward, she said it sounded like people were possessed. But we know that's not true because they are fine now. And then she said with everyone's emotions being heightened, it sounded like a spell. So I was thinking about that and how magic was sparking all around us while we were singing, and it hit me. I'm an empath. Somehow while we were singing last night, I caused everyone to go a little crazy. I think I did that and have no idea how, or why, or how to stop it in the future."

King let her words sink in for a moment before he nodded. "I think you might be right."

"Oh hell." She buried her face in her hands. "My second time singing for a crowd, and I made them go crazy."

He snorted out a laugh. "Usually that's the desired effect."

"I don't want people fighting or ripping each other's clothes off in the streets. That's insane!"

"I know." He pulled her into a hug and then looked out at the brewery. There were hardly any customers. Just her friends and Abby at the bar. It appeared that most of the town was taking it easy after the Halloween festivities. "But if it helps, I don't think it's your fault."

She pulled away from him, disentangling herself before smoothing her shirt. "How is it not my fault?"

"My mother cursed you," he blurted and then regretted it when her face went white. He wrapped his arm around her again and held on. "Take a deep breath," he coaxed. "That's it."

When color started to come back into her cheeks, she looked at him. "Your mother cursed me?" Then she frowned as her brows furrowed together. "Oh. My. Gods! She *did* curse me."

"How did she do it?" he asked.

"She shook my hand, and I felt a load of magic crawl up my arm, but then it seemed to go away. And then we went on stage, and the next thing I knew, people were losing it."

"So she shook your hand and transferred a curse," he said, wondering what kind of curse his awful mother had bestowed on her.

"I think so. Is it permanent?" she asked.

"There's only one way to find out." King took her hand in his and led her back out to the bar. "I have a favor to ask you gals."

Imogen turned to him. "And what's that?"

"Sadie thinks she cursed everyone last night, and before she freaks out too much, I'd like to do a test. I want to see if it will happen again if we sing together now."

"I'm out," Clay said from his spot behind the counter.

"I'll do it," Abby said, shooting her husband a dirty look. "This is all because you don't want that potion again, isn't it?"

"You're onto me. Sorry, King. I'm headed to the back. I wish you all the best. And if you end up spelled," he said to Imogen and Melissa, "just drink Abby's dirt juice. It really did help."

"Sounds appetizing," Melissa deadpanned. But then she looked at Sadie. "I'll do it. Just make sure I don't make a fool of myself afterward."

Sadie gave her a small smile but didn't look anywhere near pleased.

"I'll do it, too," Imogen said. "I know what it feels like to know something's off. If I can help, I will."

"Abby?" King turned to her. "Do you think you can have those potions on hand and ready to go?"

"Sure thing." Abby jumped up from the counter and retreated to the back while King led Sadie up to the stage.

He quickly went over the equipment, making sure it was set up to his satisfaction, and then he found a guitar for Sadie. They each took a stool on the stage in front of the microphone and waited until Abby returned.

Once the green juices were on the counter and the three women were seated, King signaled to Sadie to start.

Her fingers ran over the strings with expert precision, and King was both inspired and haunted by the chord progression. It was so good and so lovely that he wondered if they should put out an acoustic version.

Sadie glanced at him, and the pair of them started to sing. When King sang with her, every inch of his body felt alive. It was unlike anything he'd ever experienced with another singer. But he didn't think it had anything to do with his mother's curse. He'd felt that way even when they were seventeen and just singing softly at the beach. Whatever was between them when they sang, it was just special… as if they'd been born to be singing partners.

They were just through the first verse when King started to feel the magic creeping over his skin. It was so faint that he almost didn't notice it. But when he looked over at the bar, he could see all three of the women were in some sort of heated discussion.

King and Sadie shared a look, and by unspoken agreement, they both stopped singing and Sadie put the guitar down.

"No, that's not how you eat fries!" Abby exclaimed, pointing her finger at Melissa's plate. "Mustard should be illegal."

Melissa glared at her, picked up the mustard, and aimed.

"Stop it, you overreacting drama queen!" Imogen cried and grabbed the mustard. The two women struggled, each trying to keep control of the mustard container. They'd slid off their stools and were yanking each other back and forth, each trying to dislodge the mustard container from the other.

Abby was scowling when she tried to step in between them and stop the fight, but as soon as she reached for the container herself, one of them squeezed and the mustard sprayed all over Abby's pink *Herbs are Life* shirt.

"No!" Abby cried, wiping fruitlessly at the yellow condiment now smeared all over her shirt.

"We have to do something," Sadie insisted. "Now, before they turn this place into the mustard palace."

King nodded, and together they ran from the stage toward their friends. But when Sadie reached them, she sort of danced around them, unsure what to do.

"Abby! Imogen! Melissa!" King cried. "Stop! You don't need the mustard!"

All three of them ignored King. It wasn't until Sadie placed a hand on Melissa's back that she stopped fighting and stepped away from the other two.

"What happened?" Melissa asked as she pressed her hand to her head. "Dammit. The headache is back."

King quickly grabbed one of the potions that Abby had left on the counter and handed it to her. "Drink this. It should help."

Melissa eyed the potion and then King before she

wrinkled her nose and started to drink the green concoction. "Oh, gross. Clay is right. This does taste like dirt."

"It does not!" Abby called as she spun to look at Melissa. "It tastes like grass."

"If you say so," Melissa said.

"Got it!" Imogen held the mustard in the air, celebrating her win. But when she looked around and no one was paying her any attention, she tossed it back onto the bar and took a seat, looking a little unsure of herself.

"Here, drink this," Sadie said, putting a potion into Imogen's hand. Then she handed the final one to Abby.

Once the potions were sucked down, their three test subjects just sat at the bar in the brewery, looking a lot worse for wear.

"I guess that answers some questions," King said.

All four women looked at him, fire in their expressions.

He backed away with his hands up and then met Sadie's gaze. "I think we need to go see the healer."

"Yeah. We do." Sadie hugged each of her friends, thanked them for being her test subjects, and told them she'd keep them updated.

Melissa hugged her fiercely and held on as they had a whispered conversation.

"King?" Imogen said as she walked over to him.

"Yeah?"

"If the healer doesn't give you any answers, let me know. My sister Harlow isn't just a medium. She also understands curses and how to neutralize them. It's often the only way to send a ghost back to where they belong."

"That's… absolutely terrifying," King said. "But in a good way."

Imogen laughed. "You had it right the first time."

"I'm ready," Sadie said, appearing by King's side. He glanced at Abby and Melissa. Both seemed to be all right but still a little green around the edges. But he supposed that was inevitable when someone drank a bottle of grass potion.

"Are they okay?" King asked her.

"They are. It's just that they weren't expecting to go crazy over a bottle of mustard."

"Who would?" he asked, not expecting an answer, but he was gratified when she snickered.

CHAPTER 23

Sadie sat in King's Jeep feeling as if she wanted to climb out of her own skin. Now that she knew she was cursed, she just felt tainted. Wrong. Dirty.

"We're going to figure this out," King said, reaching across the console to take her hand.

She stared at the connection and almost pulled away, afraid she'd taint him, too. But then she remembered the night they'd shared and decided it was way too late for that. So instead, she held on tight, clinging to him as if he were a lifeline.

"I'm sure the healer will have some answers for us." King pulled into a parking spot in front of the Keating Hollow healer's office.

Before Sadie could even get unbuckled, King was opening her door and holding his hand out to her.

"I'm not disabled, you know," she said with a tired smile.

"And people wonder why chivalry is dead," he joked.

Sadie took his hand, letting him help her climb out of the Jeep. "Thanks."

"Always." King kept a tight grip on her hand as they walked into the healer's office.

"Good afternoon," the vibrant, redheaded receptionist said with a friendly smile. "What brings you in today?"

"My mother cursed my girlfriend," King said. "We want to know if the healer can help."

Girlfriend? Sadie thought. When had he decided she was his girlfriend? Then she remembered what he'd said last night before they'd given themselves to each other. *If we take this step, you're mine, Sadie Lewis.* Her heart felt as if it was going to explode.

"Sadie?" King said, sounding as if it wasn't the first time he'd tried to get her attention while standing at the desk.

"Yeah?" she answered, glancing between him and the receptionist.

"Bethany has some questions," King said.

"Right." She turned her attention to the woman behind the desk.

Bethany went through a bunch of questions about her basic health and then had her fill out a questionnaire. Once Sadie was done, she watched the woman disappear into the back. She turned to King. "Do you really think there's anything they can do?"

"We're about to find out." He led her to the waiting area, but just as they were about to sit, Bethany was back.

"You're in luck. Healer Whipple is running ahead of schedule today and said she can squeeze you in now. Come with me." Bethany held the door open for them.

Sadie stood, but when King stayed seated, she blinked at him. "Aren't you coming?"

"If you want me to," he said. "I didn't want to assume anything."

She held her hand out. "I definitely want my boyfriend with me."

He smiled softly, took her hand, and followed her into the exam room.

"Healer Whipple will be here shortly." Bethany closed the door, leaving them in the white sterile room.

"So this is weird, right?" Sadie said, still feeling like an alien in her own skin.

"Less weird than my mother cursing you as a form of blackmail," he said darkly.

"Good point."

"Hello," Healer Whipple said as she glided into the room with a warm smile on her face. She had short gray hair and kind eyes. "Sadie, it's good to see you again."

"You, too," Sadie said. "I wish we were meeting under better circumstances."

"That's always the case, dear." She turned to King. "We haven't met. I'm Healer Whipple."

"King McGrath."

They shook hands and then the healer turned back to Sadie. "It says here you think you've been cursed. Can you tell me about that?"

Sadie took a few minutes to give her the details of everything they knew, including that they thought King's mom was the caster and the spell placed on unsuspecting listeners seemed to be temporary at best.

"Okay. Let's see what we're dealing with," Healer Whipple said, taking Sadie's hand in hers. She ran her fingertips over Sadie's palm and then up and down her forearm. The healer frowned and then muttered a word that sounded like Latin. Magic sparked from Healer Whipple's fingertips and skittered over Sadie's skin, engulfing her hand and forearm.

After a moment, Sadie's skin turned bright red from her hand up to just below her elbow.

The healer looked up. "There's definitely a curse here. You said this was the hand that King's mom touched just before you felt the magic?"

"Yes," Sadie said.

"Okay. Now that we know we're dealing with a curse, tell me a little more. It only affects other people when you sing?" the healer asked, making a note on the chart.

"Yes," Sadie said with a nod. "It's when I feel emotions most intensely, so I think that might be connected."

"Interesting." The healer tilted her head to the side as she contemplated something. "That means the curse might kick in at other times besides when you sing. I think it's possible this could happen if you're going through an emotional time, too. So that's something to watch out for."

"You can't be serious," Sadie said with a sinking heart. "You mean if I'm having a bad day, I could just be walking around casting spells on people without even knowing it?"

"Or a really good day," she said. "You're happy when singing, right?"

"Dammit." Sadie glanced at King and then felt a faint brush of his guilt prick her arms. "It's not your fault," she said. "Your mother is the only one to blame."

He pressed his lips into a thin line and glanced away briefly before giving her the tiniest of nods.

"She's right, you know," the healer said. "You are not responsible for how your parents behave. Now, let's see if we have anything that can counteract this curse." She got up and went to a leatherbound book that sat on a shelf above a computer. After flipping to the index, she found the page she wanted. A moment later, she snapped it shut and replaced it on the shelf. When she turned around, she said, "Hmm. I'm not sure this is exactly what we're looking for."

Sadie's chest tightened as tears stung her eyes. Finally, just when everything in her life was falling into place, she ended up cursed. If they didn't find a way to reverse it, what would happen to her singing career? And what would happen to her and King when he went out on the road to promote, but she was back in Keating Hollow, slinging beers. Bitterness set in, and she slumped back in her chair.

"Let's give a potion a try. If it doesn't work, I'll do some research and see if we can find something else that will reverse the effects," Whipple said.

"What if you can't find anything?" King asked.

She turned her attention to King, her expression serious. "The best way to neutralize a curse is to find the person who cast it and either get them to remove it or force them to. Unfortunately, most times it's nearly impossible to find someone who is willing to admit guilt for such a thing since it's a felony in this state. If they are caught, there is mandatory jail time depending on the severity of the curse."

"Jail." He nodded. "It's what they deserve."

"Indeed. I'll be right back." The healer left the room.

Sadie stared at King, her body numb with shock at his statement. Then her heart started to ache. She'd never understand what it was like to have a mother like Cindy. And it killed Sadie that Cindy had kicked King out of the house as a teenager and then pretended he didn't exist until he had something she wanted. No wonder he was resigned to seeing her jailed. Would Sadie have felt the same way about her father if he'd managed to steal her house?

Yes. Yes she would. And the thought nearly broke her.

"We'll find her either way, Sadie," King said. "Whether

this potion works or not, I'm not letting her get away with this. It's beyond time that she faced the consequences of her actions."

"I know," Sadie said. He was right. This went beyond Cindy's heinous crime of cursing Sadie. She was also blackmailing King, and the sooner she was held accountable the better.

The door opened and Healer Whipple slipped back into the room. She was holding a quart of green-colored liquid. "This is the potion. The instructions are to drink half now and the other half first thing in the morning. Give it a full twenty-four hours for it to work. You should feel the curse detaching from your body by this time tomorrow. Once it's fully free, it will poof into a ball of smoke and your skin will go back to its normal color. If twenty-four hours pass and you don't feel anything different, we'll know it didn't work."

"How confident are you that this might clear the curse?" King asked.

"Honestly? Maybe 30%. I'll start researching after my last appointment today." Healer Whipple walked to the door. "Take your time. I know it's a lot to process. If you have questions, let Bethany know. She'll come find me. Otherwise, call tomorrow afternoon and update me on the status of your condition."

Condition, Sadie thought bitterly. That was one way to put it.

"Thank you," King said. "We appreciate your help."

"Oh, one more thing." She tapped the chart in her hand. "You're going to need to file a police report. Grab a copy of my diagnosis on the way out. The sheriff is going to need it."

"I will." Sadie straightened her shoulders, ready to file

that police report. At least then she'd feel like she was doing something.

The healer nodded curtly and slipped out of the room.

King gestured to the potion in Sadie's hand. "Bottoms up."

Sadie swallowed the lump in her throat and then downed half the potion. It tasted like bitter sour apple, and when she swallowed the last of her dose, she grimaced and said, "I'm going to need ice cream. Or chocolate. Or pie. Now."

King chuckled softly as he placed his hand on the small of her back and led her out the door. "That I can handle."

CHAPTER 24

"Chocolate caramel pie with a cookie crust!" Sadie exclaimed as she stared into the case at A Spoon Full of Magic. "I think I've died and gone to heaven." She peered at the nametag of the pretty brunette behind the counter. "Two please, Scarlet." She turned to King. "What are you having?"

"Chocolate caramel pie with a cookie crust?" he asked, assuming that second slice she'd ordered was for him.

Sadie turned back to Scarlet. "Make that three, please."

"Three?" King asked with a laugh. "Who's the third one for?"

"You, of course. You didn't think I was going to share mine, did you? One of mine is for now. The other is for later. So if you want more than one, speak up now."

"Nah, but we should get something for Briggs." King couldn't help grinning. Sadie was everything he could have asked for and more. She'd just had it confirmed that she'd been cursed by his mother, yet here she was, giddy in the enchanted sweet shop. He knew she was still freaked out, but the fact that she was still able to enjoy the moment touched him deep in his soul. He scanned the case and said, "Double Mocha Crunch. One, please."

"You got it, gorgeous," Scarlet said, giving him a quick wink before she got busy packing their pie slices.

King swallowed a groan. He was used to people flirting with him, but he wasn't a fan of the overtness right in front of Sadie.

Sadie raised her eyebrows at him. "Does that happen all the time?"

He shrugged. "Not *all* the time."

"Often enough," Sadie muttered.

"Are you two together?" Scarlet asked, sounding surprised as she looked back and forth between them.

"Yes," King said as he wrapped an arm around Sadie's shoulders and pulled her into him.

"Oh." Scarlet's eyes were wide when she added, "I'm soooo sorry." Her face flushed red. "None of the gossip sites have reported a girlfriend. I wouldn't have—never mind. I just didn't know." She glanced at Sadie. "My apologies."

Sadie handed over a credit card to pay for the purchases. "Don't worry about it. At least you aren't stalking him."

The bell over the door rang as three college-age women hurried in. One of them had thick black hair and was filming with a camera phone while the other two chattered on about Keating Hollow and how you just never knew who you were going to meet in the enchanted town.

The tall blonde who was doing most of the talking suddenly turned around and let out a loud, exaggerated gasp. "Oh. Em. Gee. Look who we found!"

Immediately King took a step back, wondering if there was a back door they could escape through.

"It's King McGrath!" Both of the women ran to either side of him and posed as if giving him a kiss on the cheek.

King was stiff with a pasted-on fake smile. "Hello, ladies. It's nice to meet you, but we're just heading out." He tried to brush past them, but one grabbed his wrist, stopping him.

Sadie stepped in and gave the woman a tight smile. She held her purchases up and said, "We're done here, so like he said, we're leaving."

"But my audience is dying to meet King. That new song of his is *fire*," the blonde said, practically leering at King.

His patience was already running on low. There was no way he could indulge this today, and he didn't even want to try. "*Our* song," King said, gesturing to Sadie. "If it weren't for Sadie, that song wouldn't exist."

"Sure. But tell us what your plans are next, King. Your audience is dying to know." The blonde batted her eyelashes at him, making him want to roll his eyes.

Why couldn't he have even ten minutes in the sweet shop without dealing with this garbage?

Sadie slipped her arm through King's and cleared her throat. In her no-nonsense voice, she said, "Sorry, ladies. But King has somewhere to be."

The raven-haired one with the camera phone moved right in front of Sadie, blocking her path to the door.

"You're going to need to move now." Sadie's tone was full of ice as magic radiated from her and settled over the store.

"Oh, come on," the blonde said, sounding impatient now. "I need this content for all the braindead McGrath fans to keep my engagement up. Don't you understand that's how I make a living? With brands overpaying me to just say I'm using their product? It would take nothing for King McGrath to do me a solid so I can get paid."

The two sidekicks both gasped out loud.

The blonde clamped her hand over her mouth and shook her head as she whispered to her friend with the camera, "You're not live, are you?"

The raven-haired friend nodded, her complexion turning green.

The third, shorter woman threw her head back and laughed. She laughed so hard that tears streamed down her cheeks. "Oh, this is delicious. Wait until the group chat hears about this."

"What group chat?" Blondie demanded.

"The secret one we named *Off with Her Head* because you act like you think you're a queen and treat the rest of us like your subjects." She was still laughing when she left the shop, already texting.

Blondie turned on the raven-haired friend. "Are you a part of that text group?"

The other woman nodded and bit down on her bottom lip but then blurted, "It's your own fault. You don't always have to be such a bitch!"

Blondie's face turned beet red, and King thought for a moment that her head might actually explode. But before he could witness such a wonderful and gruesome sight, she let out a loud groan of frustration and then stomped out of the store.

The remaining woman turned to King. "Sorry about that. I'm guessing Hailee's social media career might be on hold for a while." Snickering to herself, she walked out, leaving them alone with Scarlet.

"Whoa," Scarlet said. "That was quite the shitshow."

King nodded. "It always is."

Sadie turned to him, a sick expression on her face. "I

didn't mean to do that."

"I know."

"Wait!" Scarlet exclaimed. "*You're* responsible for causing those obnoxious girls to let their guards down and say what was on their minds?"

"It appears so," Sadie said, looking at the angry red skin on her right arm.

"Good. They got what they deserved," Scarlet said with conviction. "Those three and their friends have been the biggest pains in the ass since they arrived in town, looking for free samples all the time as they record their content. I've never met more shallow people in my life."

Sadie raised her eyebrows. "I bet you didn't mean to tell me all that."

Scarlet's lips turned up into a sheepish smile. "No, but it's one hundred percent true."

King nodded to her. "Thanks, Scarlet. You're right; they got what they deserved." He slipped his fingers through Sadie's and said, "It's time to find the sheriff."

"I guess it is," Sadie said and followed him out the door.

∼

"Hello there, King, Sadie," Clarissa, the desk clerk at the sheriff's department, said with a warm smile. "You two certainly are making news here in Keating Hollow lately."

"We are?" King asked. They hadn't done much except sing at the festival. And while the audience had gone batshit after the spell was cast on them, neither of them had stuck around long enough to be included in the town gossip, which hadn't yet connected Sadie to the spell.

"Oh yeah. Haven't you seen the viral TikTok video?" She

produced her phone and tapped a few times before handing it to King.

He stared at the video of him and Sadie at A Spoon Full of Magic. Sadie was seen telling the college girls that they needed to move, but that wasn't what made the video go viral. It was the very visible magic that seeped from Sadie's cursed hand and wrapped around the women, making them glow as they spewed their truths. Dread coiled in King's gut. This was going to be a nightmare.

Sadie, who was watching over his shoulder, let out a gasp as she clutched his arm. "That's... crazy."

"It is pretty nuts," Clarissa said. "But one thing's for sure, that song of yours? It's going to break records after this."

King didn't care about that. All he wanted was for Sadie to be free of this nightmare. He cleared his throat. "Can we speak to Sheriff Baker?"

"I'm right here." Drew Baker appeared from the closed door behind Clarissa and added, "Come on back. I just got a call from Healer Whipple, and it appears we have a situation on our hands."

"We do." King took Sadie's hand and together they made their way into the sheriff's office.

Once they were seated, the sheriff leaned forward and said, "Healer Whipple says you've been cursed and that she's verified it."

Sadie nodded and showed him her red arm. "It happened last night at the festival just before we went on stage." She told him about her encounter with Cindy and then described how the crowd reacted.

The entire time King listened to her talk, he became more and more agitated. It was one thing for his mother to target him, but to go after Sadie? She'd crossed a line she could

SONG OF THE WITCH

never come back from. When Sadie was done talking, King relayed the scene from A Spoon Full of Magic and told him to ask Clarissa to see the video.

Drew was silent through the entire exchange while he scribbled notes on a yellow legal pad. Finally he looked up and said, "There's no question you've been cursed. But is there any proof that Cindy McGrath was the one who cast the curse?"

"I told you I felt magic crawl up my arm when she touched me," Sadie said.

He nodded. "I've got that. But lots of people who have magic aren't cursing people. We'll need to match her magical signature to know for sure." He turned to King. "We can list her as a possible person of interest, but unless there's more evidence, we don't really have anything we can use to compel her to take the test. If we had more evidence, another witness or motive—"

"She left me a blackmail note!" King blurted. "She left it on my front door. It said if I'd send her the money she asked for she'd make sure my girlfriend recovered from her 'unfortunate malady.' That was right after the show."

Drew pursed his lips and nodded very slowly. "That is probably enough to issue an arrest warrant. Do you still have the letter?"

"Yes. It's at home," King said, relieved he was willing to do something.

"We're going to need that for evidence. Bring it by as soon as you can."

"I will do that later today. Thank you," King said as Sadie slumped into the chair, looking exhausted.

"I'm going to have Clarissa type up your statements. If you can both just sign them before you go, then we can get down to business." He called Clarissa in and handed her the legal pad. Once she was gone, he said, "Be sure to tell me when your mother contacts you again. We won't let this go. No one is going to get away with terrorizing our Keating Hollow family."

"Thank you, Sheriff Baker," King said, shaking the man's hand. He knew that if this had happened in LA, they wouldn't have been receiving this type of help. It was looking more and more like maybe he should move to Keating Hollow permanently. He glanced at Sadie and decided then and there that he would not be going anywhere.

"Yes, thank you, Drew," Sadie echoed, sounding weary. "I hope you find her sooner rather than later."

"I'm right there with you, Sadie." The sheriff walked them back out to the reception area and said he'd be in touch.

As they were signing their statements, both Sadie's and King's phones dinged with a text. King scanned the message on his phone and felt dread in his gut. It was Austin, and he had called them both in for an emergency meeting.

Sadie stared at the phone for a long moment before she took a deep breath and walked out of the station. King hurried after her, wishing there was something, *anything*, he could do to make this easier for her. He wrapped an arm around her shoulders and said, "We'll find my mother and turn her in. One way or another, we're going to fix this."

She met his gaze and said, "I know. I just hope it isn't too late."

"Too late for what?" he asked.

Sadie held her phone up, showing him a reel that was a conspiracy theory of the video of her spelling the women at A Spoon Full of Magic. Right across the top it said, *Don't be fooled by a witch. Zero musical talent. You've been duped.*

King scowled. "Forget these people, Sadie. Seriously. People will post anything for clicks and clout these days. We know our song is special. And so do millions of other people who have already streamed it."

"I hope you're right. People have been canceled for less." She walked over to the Jeep and climbed in.

King muttered a prayer to the internet gods. "Please don't let this take on a life of its own. Not now. Not ever."

As he got into the Jeep and saw Sadie still scrolling on her phone while she chewed nervously on her bottom lip, he knew his prayer was wasted.

There was no controlling a narrative once the damage had been done.

It appeared they were too late.

CHAPTER 25

All Sadie wanted to do was go home and bury herself in her covers with Cosmo by her side. Instead, she was walking into Austin's office to learn about the fate of her fledgling singing career.

"There you are," Austin said, ushering them in. "It's been quite the day, hasn't it?"

"I guess you could say that," Sadie said, taking a seat in a chair across from his desk.

"It's been a lot," King agreed as he stood behind Sadie's chair and placed his hands on her shoulders, kneading gently.

Sadie closed her eyes briefly, grateful for his touch. She hadn't realized just how tense she was until right that minute.

"First the good news," Austin said. "The song is breaking records climbing the charts. It's number one on multiple streaming stations and is trending on TikTok. You both should be really proud of yourselves."

King reached for Sadie's hand, and she smiled at him as their fingers entwined.

Austin watched the interaction and raised one eyebrow. "Are you two an item now?"

Sadie and King nodded at the same time.

"All right." Austin didn't look terribly pleased at the pairing, but he kept his thoughts to himself. There was nothing in the contracts that said two artists couldn't date each other. Sadie assumed he just didn't want the added headache. "I've got a number of appearances set up for both of you. You'll need to decide whether you want to disclose your relationship to the public or not."

"I'm not keeping it a secret," King said. "I don't care who knows."

Sadie grimaced. She hadn't thought about what it would mean to tell the world about her and King, but she agreed. She couldn't keep him a secret. He was important to her, and if it meant one less person harassed him because they knew he was taken, then it was worth it.

"Okay, we'll get a story out there soon, so we can control the narrative. After today's viral video, I think most people won't be surprised. Sadie, you're turning into something of a legend after you stepped in to protect King from invasive fans," Austin said, smiling at her. "Some are even saying you're a hero. No one likes a fake social media influencer."

"That's…" Sadie shook her head. "I don't know what to say to that."

He shrugged. "It's better than the alternative, I suppose. It's certainly not hurting sales or streaming numbers. So let's not worry about that for now. Let's talk about the appearances I have scheduled for you two over the next few weeks. There's a couple of late-night talk shows, a podcast, a morning show, music interviewers." Austin sat back and smiled. "You name it, we've got someone trying to get access."

"I can't do any live shows," Sadie said. "Not while I'm carrying around this curse."

"Curse? What curse?" Austin stood with his hands balled into fists at his waist. "What did I miss?"

"You didn't think I spelled those girls on purpose, did you?" Sadie asked, shocked. "I'd never do something like that."

Austin cringed. "I used to live in LA, Sadie. I've seen it all. Now someone tell me about this curse."

King told him the entire story and concluded with the sheriff issuing a warrant for Cindy's arrest.

"Your mother did this?" Austin looked like he was ready to explode. "Your own mother?"

"Yes. The worst part is I'm not even that surprised," King said.

Sadie turned sharply to look at King. "You're not surprised she cursed someone? Has she done this before?"

"No, no. Not that I know of, anyway." King waved his hands as if clearing the air in front of him. "I had no idea she'd do this. I just mean that nothing she does surprises me anymore."

"Right. Of course." Sadie was just so tired she wasn't thinking straight. Maybe the potion the healer had given her was starting to do its job. "Austin, listen, I'm nowhere near ready to sing for an audience right now. If I end up casting a spell on them because of this curse, I'll never forgive myself. I just can't risk it. Right now, we think it affects people temporarily, but we just can't be sure, and I don't want to take any chances." She chewed on her bottom lip for a moment before adding, "If you have to replace me on the record, I understand."

"Replace you?" Austin asked at the same time King said, "That's not going to happen."

"I just don't want to stand in the way of the obvious success of the song," Sadie said, trying to hold back tears. "I can't perform, so I can't promote. And I know that's part of the deal. No one gets to sit in a studio and just push music out without touring and promoting it."

"Sadie," Austin said as he got up from his chair and walked to stand in front of her. He leaned against the desk and met her gaze. "You're not going anywhere."

"But I can't—" she started to protest, but Austin held his hand up, stopping her.

"You are a part of this team and a vital part of the success of this song. You're not going to be dropped because you've been targeted by a criminal. That's not how I do things, and I'm certain that King wouldn't stand for that either."

"Nope," King said, crossing his arms over his chest.

"We're a family here. And in this family, we take care of each other."

Sadie stared at Austin, her heart beating too fast as emotion overwhelmed her. She stared at her red hand and said, "If I stay here in this office any longer, I might end up spelling you, too. I'm about five seconds from crying."

"It's okay, Sadie," Austin said kindly. "I promise, these are my real feelings. If I'm cursed to let my guard down, you're more likely to get a sappier version of me. So my apologies in advance to you."

That made her laugh. And then she smiled back. "Thank you."

"We'll hold off on the in-person appearances. Maybe set

up a couple of remote ones where you and King can perform. And then we'll take it from there. Okay?"

Sadie nodded and then looked over at King.

"You can't get rid of me now," he said with a cocky smile.

"Good, because I really love this song and working with both of you," Sadie said. "So thank you for talking me down."

"Go get some rest," Austin said. "I have phone calls to make."

Sadie stood on shaky legs and was grateful when King slipped his arm around her. She leaned into him, and for the first time since she'd lost her grandmother, she felt like she had someone other than Melissa and Rachel to call family.

∼

SADIE LISTENED to the soft snores from Cosmo as she stared at the ceiling. King was passed out, sleeping soundly, while she hadn't slept a wink. When they'd gotten back to Brigg's house that day, King had run out to deliver the blackmail note to the sheriff while she'd busied herself making dinner. She'd needed something to keep her mind off the day. And then when it came time to eat the lasagna she finally got around to making, she'd sat at the table, barely touching anything.

It wasn't long after that when she'd given up and gone to bed.

King had come with her, saying he just wanted to hold her while she went to sleep. Too bad his plan hadn't worked. While he'd drifted off relatively soon, it was three hours later and her mind was still racing.

Being careful to not wake King or Cosmo, Sadie silently slipped from the bed and padded into the kitchen. After making herself a cup of tea, she retrieved one of her pieces of the chocolate caramel pie she'd purchased earlier in the day. After the incident at the shop and meeting with the sheriff, she just hadn't been hungry. But chocolate was definitely in order now.

Sadie had just taken the first bite of her pie when she heard faint footsteps and looked up to see a rumpled Briggs walk into the kitchen. "Hey," she said. "Can't sleep?"

"Nope." He ran a hand through his messy hair as he eyed her pie. "That looks good."

"There's another piece in the fridge with your name on it." Sadie should have known that her eyes were bigger than her stomach when she'd bought two slices for herself. It never failed that she overpurchased her favorite desserts and then was never able to eat it all. Better too much than not enough, right?

"Thanks." He got the second slice of pie and a cup of decaf coffee and joined her at the table. "What has you up in the middle of the night?"

"Nothing. Everything." She gave him a weak smile. "You know how it is. The brain can't shut off sometimes."

He let out a humorless laugh. "Yeah. I know that feeling all too well."

"Want to talk about it?" she asked, ready to focus on someone else for a while.

"No." He snorted and then took a bite of the pie. "My god, Sadie. This is sinful."

"Isn't it, though?" She took another small bite and let the sweetness melt over her tongue. "Why can't things like this be good for our health? We'd all live to be a hundred and twenty."

"Who wants that?" Briggs asked.

"Uh, happy people?" she guessed, and then looked at him closer. He had bags under his eyes, and he looked like he hadn't slept in days. "Briggs, what's wrong?"

"Nothing," he said too quickly.

She raised both eyebrows. "You don't have to tell me, but maybe talk to King about whatever it is, okay? Because it's obvious something is up."

"He's the last person I'd talk to about this." Briggs sat back and closed his eyes. "Not now. Not with everything going on with his mother. I don't want to make his situation all about me."

"What do you mean, all about you? Has Cindy approached you, too?" Sadie asked, worried that she'd somehow pulled Briggs into her devious plans.

"No, no. Nothing like that." He shook his head and then sighed. "All this crap with King and his mom... It just serves as a reminder of my own family garbage I had to deal with before I ended up in foster care. You know, childhood trauma and all that bullshit. Don't worry about it. I'll be fine."

Sadie met his gaze and said, "You know it's okay to not be fine, right?"

"Not to me," he said and got up to take his empty plate to the sink. "The sooner I can forget the better."

"Briggs?"

He paused and glanced back at her.

"I'm here if you ever need to talk. I'm not King, but... I've had my own issues to deal with. I can listen if nothing else."

He stared down at his feet before giving her a nod. "Thanks, Sadie. I appreciate that."

Sadie watched as the man rubbed the back of his neck and disappeared down the hallway. She eyed her half-eaten pie, put it back in the refrigerator, and took herself back to bed. Once she was under the covers, she rolled over and placed her head on King's chest.

Cosmo resettled himself right next to her and as she concentrated on the soft sounds of his breathing, this time she fell into a deep dreamless sleep.

CHAPTER 26

King paced the living room as he tried not to watch the clock. In just two more minutes, they'd know if the potion that Healer Whipple has prescribed had worked or not. It had been just about twenty-four hours since the first dose Sadie had taken in her office and about eight since she'd taken the second dose.

The clock on the wall ticked.

Sadie and King stared at each other.

Tick. Tick. Tick.

Five minutes went by and then ten. Nothing happened. Sadie's hand and arm were still red. The puff of smoke Healer Whipple had described never happened.

Sadie sighed and flopped down on the couch. She picked up her phone and called the healer, leaving a message to let them know the potion didn't work. After she ended the call, she said, "I guess we shouldn't be too surprised. Healer Whipple said it was a longshot at best."

"I guess you're right," King agreed, but as he continued to pace the living room, his ire grew. He had to do something.

Anything. He knew he couldn't just let this be while his mother was out plotting more ways to mess with his life. He grabbed his phone and hit her number.

"Kevin. I've been waiting to hear from you," she said coolly.

"I just bet you have." He didn't bother to hide his anger. "Not looking to earn that mother of the year award, are you?"

She laughed. "You always were a dramatic child. Always getting upset after you eavesdropped on people's private thoughts. I figured you of all people would like it when someone was honest. That way you wouldn't have to skulk around their inner thoughts like a creeper."

King hated the woman on the other end of the line with the force of a thousand suns. He wasn't anything to her but a meal ticket, and they both knew it. The days of him trying to salvage some sort of relationship with her just because she'd given him life were long gone. "Where can I meet you? I'll give you your damned money but only if you neutralize that curse you cast on Sadie."

"I knew you'd see it my way." Her tone was dripping with condescension.

"The money in exchange for leaving us alone," he said.

"Fine. But the price just went up to one hundred thousand because you went to the police. How many times have I told you that family never narcs on family?"

"And what if I don't have a hundred thousand dollars?" He did, but that money was tied up in his retirement account. Contrary to what she thought, he didn't have a limitless bank account.

"Then that curse your girlfriend has will continue to get

worse. If you think it's bad now, just wait until people start acting out every vile and evil thought they have after being around her. It will be her fault when that sappy little town you're staying in right now ends up being a horror show that no one ever visits because everyone has become the most toxic versions of themselves. On the other hand, that would make one hell of a reality show. You should get in on that before someone else does. You can thank me by paying fifty percent royalties."

King pulled the phone away from his ear and stared at it, wondering if his mother had been possessed.

But when he put the phone back to his ear, she said, "Remember when that neighbor crashed into your dad's car and then refused to pay for the damages?"

"You mean when dad cut him off and was T-boned?" King said, knowing that his dad was one hundred percent at fault for that accident.

"He had the right of way," she insisted. "Anyway, he refused, so I cursed him with a bad luck money spell. Do you know where that neighbor is now?"

King gritted his teeth and said nothing. He didn't want to know.

"He's living in a broken-down camper on his daughter's property without a dime to his name. Turns out he should have just paid for the car he smashed up, don't you think?"

His mother was truly evil. There was no other way to put it. "I just want this behind us. You come here and neutralize Sadie's curse, and I'll get you your money."

She let out a bark of laughter. "You think I'm going anywhere near you? Think again, little narc. I'll text you an address and a time. But I warn you... If you involve any law enforcement in this, you won't like what happens next."

The call ended and King squeezed the phone so hard he was surprised it didn't shatter right there in his hand.

"You're not really going to pay her, are you?" Sadie asked, studying him with concern in her gaze.

"I'll do what I have to in order to end this mess," he said.

"King, you can't keep giving her money," Sadie insisted.

He turned to stare at her. "Sadie, you don't know what she's capable of. I will not risk you for anything, let alone money. Do you understand? I couldn't live with myself if I just let this go. I have to finish this with her. Somehow, some way, it's got to end."

She blinked rapidly at him. "You are going to call Sheriff Baker, aren't you?"

"Yes. Of course. But I want to find out where she is first, get a read on her before I call in the cops. She'll flee the moment she suspects them. I just wish I had some idea how to do that."

Sadie let out a long breath. "I think I know someone who can help."

He raised his eyebrows. "Who?"

"Imogen's sister." Sadie grabbed her phone and made the call.

~

KING CHECKED his phone for what felt like the thousandth time. His mother still hadn't sent him a meetup point or instructions for whatever she had planned. Not that it mattered. If he had his way, he'd know where she was within the hour anyway.

Sadie pulled her car into a long driveway in front of a large farmhouse out in the woods. The pretty porch was

SONG OF THE WITCH

decorated with pumpkins and gourds and a fall wreath. It looked just like all the other carefully cared for homes in Keating Hollow. Peaceful. Welcoming. Homey.

All it did was make King more determined to stop the madness his mother was promising. He'd come to love Keating Hollow in the short time that he'd been there. The thought of his mother ruining it to fill some deep hole in her soul was unacceptable. He'd no sooner risk the town than he would Sadie's wellbeing.

"Hey," Imogen said as she stepped out onto the porch. "Harlow and Cash are inside getting the circle ready for you."

"Thanks, Imogen," Sadie said, giving her friend a hug. "I appreciate you setting this up for us."

"There's no guarantees. And ghosts do lie sometimes, so take it all with a grain of salt, okay?" She glanced back at the house with a worried expression. "Why don't you two go on in. I'm going to take off."

"You're not staying?" King asked.

"Ghosts really aren't my thing. At all," Imogen said and then hurried over to a green Jeep and took off, spinning the wheels like she couldn't get out of there fast enough.

"I guess she really doesn't like ghosts," King said.

"That's an understatement," Sadie said as she knocked on the screen door.

"Come on in," Harlow called from inside.

King followed Sadie into the house and stopped dead in his tracks when he saw a giant salt circle and what seemed like a hundred candles all set up in the room. There was a pentagram in the middle of the circle as well as a bowl with a sage stick.

"Welcome," Harlow said as she hugged Sadie and then

held her hand out to King. "It's nice to finally meet you. I did hear your song. It's really something special."

"Thanks," King said. "We like to think so."

Cash walked up behind her and shook King's hand, too. "Sorry to hear about the trouble with your mom. But hopefully we can get some answers for you today."

King thanked them. Harlow and Cash were an attractive couple who seemed to move in sync with each other. It was the type of teamwork that made him think that they'd been doing this a long time. It was also obvious by the way they were always touching, either in passing or while standing next to each other, that they were crazy about each other. It's what King wanted for him and Sadie.

"Okay," Harlow said to King. "So we're going to ask our guides and yours to chime in and let us know if they can pinpoint where your mother is."

"Guides?" he asked. While King was familiar with spells and potions, ghosts weren't really something he'd paid much attention to. As far as he knew, he didn't have any medium abilities.

"Yes, your spirit guides. Whoever watches over you in the afterlife. Hopefully, we can contact them and they'll have something to tell us today."

"Okay. What do you need me to do?"

Harlow gestured to the circle. "Stand in the middle of the pentagram. Did you bring something that can connect us to your mother?"

He pulled the envelope she'd taped to Brigg's door out of his pocket. While he'd taken the letter to the sheriff, he'd left the envelope on his dresser and was grateful he'd still had it.

"This is her handwriting?" Harlow asked.

He nodded.

"Perfect. Okay, take your place." She turned to Sadie. "We'll want you to stand on the circle with us. Do you have much magic?"

"A little. I'm an empath, so I don't do spells or anything," she said.

"No problem. That will do."

Harlow led Sadie to her spot on the circle and then Harlow and Cash formed sort of a triangle.

Both Harlow and Cash picked up the candles at their feet and indicated that Sadie should do the same. Cash met King's gaze. "You just hold that envelope. We'll do the rest."

"Okay." King stood in the center of the circle and waited as magic started to swirl around him.

Harlow and Cash both chanted, "Spirits of the shadow world, we seek guidance from our loved ones. We need help finding a path. We seek knowledge and peaceful contact."

The magic became more intense as it crawled all over King's body, sparking with tiny pricks of light.

"We offer our love with only good intentions," Harlow called out. "Please help guide us to the one we seek. The offering is given freely. It's only knowledge we seek."

The candles flickered and the floorboards creaked. An eerie otherworldly feeling consumed King, and he had the intense desire to bolt from the house. Summoning ghosts definitely hadn't been on his bucket list.

The envelope flew out of his hand and shot straight up in the air, flipping and turning all different directions until finally floating gently down to King's feet. Once it hit the hardwood floor, the envelope burst into a ball of flames, quickly turning to black ash.

King stared at it, wondering if the two ghost hunters had failed. Disappointment settled in his chest, but then suddenly, just like that, a pretty female ghost with auburn hair and a kind smile appeared before him.

"Damn. You're hot," she said, eyeing King. "You can't be from Keating Hollow. I'd have remembered that handsome face and chiseled jawline."

"No, I'm new in town," King said, staring at the ghost with wide eyes. "Are you really a ghost?"

The spirit snorted. "Yes, I really am a ghost. And I was busy spying on the cast of *Island Boys* while they were filming, so this better be good." She twisted and looked at Cash. "Is he my present?"

"You've been watching too much trash television, Aunt Jane. We need a favor," Cash said.

"Of course you do, darling. That's the only reason you ring these days," she said flippantly, sounding more hurt than anything else.

"To be fair, it takes quite a bit of energy to summon you," he said impatiently. "We both know you can pop in anytime you want to."

"I know, but it's nice to be invited." She winked at Cash and then turned to Harlow. "How can I help you?"

"Not me, King," she said, gesturing to the man in the middle of the pentagram. "We need to find his mother. Can you use the ashes of the offering to find her location?"

"Is she hurt?" Aunt Jane asked, suddenly looking serious.

"No. She's hurting other people, and we need to stop her," King said.

Aunt Jane's expression turned stormy. Then the wind picked up and the ashes started flying around the circle, faster and faster, until finally Aunt Jane walked right into the windy vortex. The ashes fell to the ground again as Aunt Jane stared past King and said, "The Seacomber Inn, Room 207."

King didn't have any idea where that was, but he was sure he could find out.

Aunt Jane shook herself slightly and blinked twice. Then she looked into King's eyes and said, "Go. Now."

The air picked up in the room one more time just before Aunt Jane vanished again.

"Well, that was a success," Harlow said, grinning. "You heard Aunt Jane. Go. Now. Who knows how long your mother will be there?"

King shook Cash's hand first and then Harlow's. "Thank you. You have no idea how much I appreciate this."

"We do," Harlow said. "Now get moving. We don't want this to be for nothing."

Sadie, who'd been silent and awestruck during the entire ritual, reached out for King's hand. "Let's go."

He nodded, and together they hurried out of the house.

The moment they were back in Sadie's car, King googled the Seacomber Inn. "It's in Blue Lake. Looks like it's about twenty miles from here."

"I know the place. Hold on." Sadie made the turn onto the highway and pressed onto the gas, handling the curves like an expert. Or someone who had grown up on these roads.

King pulled his phone out and called Sheriff Baker. "We've found her." He relayed the details.

"Okay. Nice work, King. Now let us do our jobs. We'll bring her in," the sheriff said.

"We're already on our way. Besides, I want to see this."

Drew Baker put on his sheriff voice when he said, "Go home, King. Leave this to the professionals. We'll call you as soon as we have her in custody so that Healer Whipple can neutralize the curse. Understand?"

He looked at Sadie. "Sheriff Baker wants us to stand down."

"That's an order, King." The sheriff ended the call, leaving King a little bit regretful he'd called him at all.

King just had a gut feeling that they were running out of time, and he was loath to turn and run from a woman who'd been a problem his entire life. This time, he was going to get justice. Justice for Sadie, but also for the young man who'd been kicked out of Cindy's house for having an unusual ability.

"Are we turning around?" Sadie asked.

"No. I have to see this through," King said.

And much to King's surprise, Sadie just nodded and tightened her grip on the wheel as she sped along the dark mountain highway.

CHAPTER 27

"Wait here," King said as he pushed the car door open. She'd backed into a parking spot beneath a tree and between two large trucks so that her vehicle wasn't easily seen from the rest of the parking lot.

"No way. I'm going with you," Sadie insisted. She wasn't going to sit back and wait to see what happened. Wasn't she the one who was carrying around a curse?

"Sadie…" He gave her a pained look. "I don't know what we're walking into up there. I just don't want to see you hurt again."

"I get that, but you have to understand that I don't want to see you hurt either," she said.

"But she won't hurt me. I'm her cash cow."

"Dammit," she muttered and closed the car door without getting out. "You're right. She won't hurt you as long as she thinks she can get something out of you. But me—"

"She'll do anything she can think of to make sure she gets her way, which includes torturing you. I just can't let that happen," he said, shaking his head.

As much as she hated it, she understood his reasoning. Sadie nodded once and said, "I'll be here. Text me as soon as you can so I know what's happening."

King leaned across the console of her car, gave her a quick kiss, and said, "I will."

"Be safe!" she called after him and then watched as he walked up the stairs to the second floor of the motel and then down to Room 207. He knocked twice, and as he stood there waiting for the door to open, he started rocking back and forth from foot to foot.

The door finally opened, and King stepped inside.

Sadie waited for a good twenty minutes before she got out of the car and started to pace. Then suddenly, sirens filled the air as a line of three police cars sped into the parking lot. Sadie quickly got back into her car, not wanting to be a distraction for the sheriff's department.

Then she watched with rapt attention as they stormed Room 207. Her stomach churned as she worried about King, praying that he'd finally step out of the hotel room. But all she saw were the deputies milling around.

Desperate for some news, she grabbed her phone and started to text, only to be interrupted when her car door swung open. She jerked her head up and saw Cindy McGrath staring down at her.

"Cindy, where's—"

A small prick hit her neck, and suddenly Sadie's vision started to blur. "What happened?" she forced out, but she was pretty certain she'd slurred her words. A moment later, her world turned black.

SADIE WOKE IN A DARK ROOM, her head pounding. She blinked, trying to place her surroundings. Nothing was familiar, and the room smelled like moldy cheese. She groaned as she pushed herself up into a sitting position.

"Welcome back," a very unwelcome voice said from across the room.

"Where did I go?" Sadie asked, her voice so groggy she barely got the words out. She squinted, trying to take in the shabby decor. There was a fair amount of moonlight shining in the small window, illuminating the cabin's bare wood walls and rough floor. Where the hell had Cindy taken her? Deliverance county?

"Just a little nap. Nothing life-changing." Cindy stood and walked over to the small bed Sadie had been lying on. She handed Sadie a black burner phone and said, "Now, take this phone and call my son."

"Call him? Why? Are you going to let him pick me up?" Sadie asked, knowing there was no chance in hell. The events of the night were suddenly rushing back in her mind, and since Cindy had managed to somehow escape the sheriff, that meant King had been left behind. No doubt he was working with them now to find both Sadie and his mother.

"Eventually. If he gives me what I need, then yeah, he can have you back. If he doesn't, well, let's just say I'm sorry you ever got involved with my self-centered son. He never did care about anyone other than himself."

Sadie already knew that was bullshit. King loved her, and while he hadn't said it yet, she'd felt it. Knew all the way down to her toes that he cared not just for her, but for Briggs, too. It was Cindy who didn't care about anyone but herself.

"Call him," she ordered.

Sadie looked at the phone and then back at Cindy. "I don't know his number."

Cindy rolled her eyes and muttered something about lazy millennials. She punched the numbers into the phone and then handed it to Sadie.

King answered on the first ring. "Sadie? Is that you? Where are you?"

"Some cabin goddess only knows where," she said, glaring at Cindy. "With your mother."

He sucked in a sharp breath. "Has she hurt you?"

"Not after the tranquilizer she hit me with. But apparently if you don't do what she wants, she's going to take her ire out on me."

"Put her on the line," King ordered.

Sadie held the phone out to Cindy. "He wants to talk to you."

"I bet he does." But she shook her head and picked up a lead pipe. "Tell him to wire the money immediately, or I'll have no choice but to smash your fingers."

"You wouldn't dare!" Sadie said, recoiling away from the crazy person.

"Oh, I would. And I'm kind of looking forward to it. Nothing would hurt King more than crippling his new toy."

Sadie wanted to scratch her eyes out for acting as if King didn't care about her as well as threatening her hands. Sadie wouldn't be able to play the guitar for a long time if Cindy crushed her hands. Maybe never again if she was good enough at it.

"Sadie?" King called. "Any idea where the cabin is?"

"No. She has a metal pipe and is threatening to crush my fingers if you don't wire the money," Sadie said.

SONG OF THE WITCH

"Tell him to make it double. It's the fee for calling the sheriff," Cindy said.

"You're evil." Sadie glared at the woman, wondering why she'd bothered to ever have a child at all.

"Tell him."

Sadie let out a small growl but relayed the message. "She says make it double as a payback for involving the sheriff."

"She's delusional," King said softly. "But tell her I'll do it if she tells me where I can pick you up."

Sadie repeated King's demand to Cindy, who shook her head slowly. "We already tried that. I'm not falling for it again." She grabbed the phone. "Send the money and I'll let Sadie go. That's it." She shoved the phone back at Sadie.

Sadie stared at Cindy as she waited for King's response. "King? It's Sadie again. I think she's done with you."

"That's convenient, because I'm done with her as well." There was a pause and then King said, "Tell her the money will be there in ten minutes."

The moment Sadie informed Cindy of King's decision, she plucked the phone from Sadie and said, "Not a minute later. I'll send coordinates for your precious piece of ass once I'm well away from Keating Hollow."

"Don't call her that," Sadie heard King yell at his mother.

Cindy snorted her derision and ended the call. Then she smashed the burner phone and tossed it into a corner. She sat down in her chair and ignored Sadie.

"Why do you hate your son?" Sadie blurted.

Cindy blinked. "What makes you think I hate him?"

Sadie's entire body was burning with rage. "Do you need a list?"

"Just because I'm pressuring him for money doesn't mean I hate him. I love my son. But he needs to do more for his mother. He's always been a stuck-up kid, but he's a million times worse now that he's had a taste of fame."

Jealousy and resentment hit Sadie hard as Cindy rose from her chair and grabbed a small tablet from her bag. She sneered at Sadie. "Stop reading my emotions."

"I can't help it," Sadie said.

"You little liar!" Cindy grabbed her pipe and swung it at Sadie, aiming not for her hands, but her head.

Sadie rolled off the bed, her heart hammering uncontrollably as she dodged Cindy's attack. Fear had taken over, and Sadie was in full-on flight mode, only there was nowhere to go. She was pressed up against the rough wall, watching as Cindy stalked toward her, the pipe still in her right hand.

"Why are you so bitter?" Sadie shouted at her. Instantly, Sadie's arm started to tingle, and magic seeped from Sadie into Cindy, compelling her to speak her truth.

Cindy stopped and stared at Sadie for a long moment and then blurted, "You would be too if your mother locked you in the basement for most of your childhood."

Sadie let out a loud gasp. She hadn't been expecting that.

"Compared to her, I'm mother of the goddammed universe. I never did anything like that to my son even when King was assaulting my thoughts and memories. Do you have any idea what it's like to have someone pull the threads of the memories from the worst days of your life? That's why he had to go. It was either let him drive me certifiably insane or cut him off. I did what I had to do."

There were no words to describe the horror that Sadie felt for the younger version of Cindy and what she must have gone through. But Sadie would argue that the woman hadn't made it out of that in one piece. She was batshit insane, and any mother who put her own child out on the street for something he couldn't control was in serious need of therapy.

"Don't judge me, you little bitch," Cindy sneered. "Not all of us grow up in Mayberry with perfect little lives where nothing bad ever happens to them until the evil wicked witch comes to town."

Sadie didn't bother to correct her. She owed Cindy no details about her life. Instead she asked, "Where are we?"

"The woods," Cindy said as she tapped on her tablet.

"Which woods and how far from civilization?"

"None of your damned business." Cindy touched the screen on her tablet and then let out a whoop of joy. Her fingers flew over the touchscreen as she muttered to herself about multiple transfers. Then she looked up and scowled at Sadie. "Too bad. I was looking forward to breaking those fingers." She tilted her head and said, "Maybe I'll do it anyway as a reminder."

"Try it and die," Sadie hissed.

Cindy pushed her tablet into a backpack, grabbed the pipe, and walked out of the room without another word.

Sadie raced after her, took a few seconds to realize that she had absolutely no idea where she was, and then startled when she heard the roar of an ATV come to life. She knew she should let the woman drive off into the darkness. That it meant she'd no longer have to deal with her threats, but she also didn't want her getting away with all of King's money. If she wasn't stopped now, this would keep happening to King over and over and over again. Sadie had to do something.

But what?

"We can help," a very familiar and very welcome voice

said. Sadie's eyes instantly filled with tears as she recognized her mother's voice.

Sadie turned to see her mother floating next to her, with her grandmother on the other side. They were both grinning at her.

"You're so brave, honey pie," Sadie's grandmother said.

"Mom? Grandma? What are you… how did you… Why are you here?"

"You summoned us," her mother said kindly. "Now let us do what we came here to do."

Sadie wasn't sure what she meant, but in the next moment, both her grandmother and mother were standing in front of the side by side. They materialized as fully fleshed humans, causing Cindy to shriek as she swerved to keep from hitting them.

The ATV wobbled as Cindy yanked on the steering wheel, over-corrected, and ended up plowing right into a redwood.

Sadie took off at a sprint, only stopping when she got to the ATV. Cindy was trapped under it, struggling to get out of the seat. Sadie just stared down at her and shook her head. "It sucks to be the incompetent bad guy." Then she gave Cindy the widest grin and said, "Well done."

"Get this off me!" Cindy demanded.

"No way in hell," Sadie said and then patted her pockets, looking for her phone in vain. Cindy must have confiscated it when they got to the cabin. She looked at her two mother figures and asked, "Do you know where my phone is?"

Her grandmother pointed to Cindy. "In her front pocket."

"That figures." After some wrestling with her prisoner, Sadie managed to get her phone and got King on the line. "I still don't know where I am, but your mother is neutralized for now."

"What? How?" King asked, sounding shocked.

"It's a long story, but my mom and grandmother did it. True heroes. What about you? What happened when you went into that hotel room?"

He let out a growl of frustration. "My mother got me with some sleeping potion, and when I woke up, both of you were gone but the sheriff was there. I had no idea what was happening."

"She got me with the same potion," Sadie said. "If I turn on the tracking feature on my phone, can you find me?"

"I *will* find you," King promised. "Always."

"That's exactly what I needed to hear."

CHAPTER 28

Sadie was sitting on the broken-down porch, smiling with tears in her eyes. Her grandmother was on one side and her mother on the other.

"I love you, Sadie. So much. I'm very proud of who you've become," her mother said, beaming at her.

"So am I, Kitty," her grandmother said. "You always did light up a room, and now you're going to be doing it from a stage. I don't think I have ever been more impressed with a young person."

Sadie chuckled. "I'm not that young. You know that, right Gran?"

Her grandmother waved an impatient hand. "You don't have wrinkles yet. You're young. Embrace it."

All three of them laughed.

"You're going to be a huge star," Sadie's mother mused. "I can see it. Household name kind of star." She reached up a hand as if she were going to pat Sadie's arm, but in her ghostly state, it didn't work. The visit with her mother and grandmother was more than Sadie could have ever dreamed of, except for the fact that she couldn't hug either of them.

"I miss you both terribly," Sadie said.

"We know, sweetheart," her grandmother said. "But we need you to know we're always here. Always watching over you."

Her mother floated up off the porch and hovered at the end. A moment later, Sadie's grandmother did the same. They floated together in a united front as Sadie heard a Jeep engine roaring up the lane, followed by the periodic *whoop* of the sheriff's vehicle that was following it.

She felt rather than saw her mother and grandmother relax when they realized that King and the law were coming. And the closer the vehicles got, the more transparent the ghosts became.

"it's time for us to go, my love," Sadie's mother said, tears standing in her eyes. "Until we meet again. I am always here if you need me."

Sadie nodded, not bothering to try to hold back her own tears. "I love you."

"I love you too, honey." Her mother faded into the ether first, and Sadie thought her heart might shrivel and die right there. It was almost as if she were that seventeen-year-old girl all over again.

But then her grandmother spoke. "King is your soulmate, Sadie. I hope you realize that."

"Soulmate?" Sadie asked with a heavy dose of skepticism.

Her grandmother grinned and then winked as she followed her daughter's lead and vanished right before Sadie's eyes.

"Sadie!" King called as he ran from the Jeep that was parked halfway down the debris-filled driveway. He reached her and gathered her into a bear hug, gripping so tight Sadie could barely breathe. But she didn't care. King was there, and his mother was still trapped under the ATV.

"Excuse me," Sheriff Baker said, sounding very much like a disturbed lawman. "Sadie, I need a full accounting of what happened here. Also, where is Cindy McGrath?"

Sadie pointed to the woman still flailing beneath the ATV and said, "Her tablet is in her bag. Make sure you get that. She used it to make all her transfers after King paid her."

"Don't worry about that. The money is traceable and has already been intercepted," Sheriff Baker said. "She wasn't going to get far, but I do like your style, Sadie Lewis. Much more interesting than catching her at the border." He grinned and then went to deal with King's mother.

"I can't wait to get out of here," Sadie said.

But King didn't look so happy. He was staring at her arm. "She didn't fix the curse before she tried to run?"

Sadie shook her head.

"I should have known," he said. Without a word, he tugged Sadie over to the ATV and his screaming mother. Then he kneeled next to her and said, "Neutralize the curse."

"Why?" Cindy didn't even look at him.

"Because you owe it to me for being a shitty parent," King said and then stepped on her limp wrist.

Cindy let out a howl of pain.

"Want me to keep going, or are you going to neutralize the curse?"

"No!" she cried. "I mean, yes, I'll neutralize the curse."

"Good. That's what I thought you'd say," King said before holding out his hand to Sadie and tugging her over. "Right now."

"I said okay!" Cindy screamed.

King smiled and pushed Sadie forward. "Go ahead then."

Sadie didn't want to touch Cindy. Not ever again. She just didn't trust the witch. But when Cindy started to mutter phrases in Latin and Sadie could feel the cleansing energy radiating off her, she stepped in, ready to rid herself of the curse.

The moment Cindy touched Sadie, her arm turned warm with tingles crawling all over the red markings. And then abruptly the redness turned into a puff of smoke.

Sadie knew in an instant she was free of the curse and took several steps back, trying to put as much distance between her and Cindy as possible.

King noticed, came over, and wrapped his arms around her. "It's fine now, Sadie. It's over."

She buried her face in his chest and then looked up at him with a tiny smile on her lips. "And now we can have our perfect beginning."

He smiled down at her and said, "We already have." Then he bent his head, and Sadie lifted her head up, claiming his lips for her own.

∽

THE NEXT WEEK was spent doing live shows down in LA to promote Sadie and King's song. No one was affected by Sadie's magic. The song had hit the top of every chart, and Sadie and King had started to work on new music.

They had just walked into Brigg's house and found Briggs and Cosmo on the floor. Cosmo had his paws up in the air, being a whore for the belly rubs Briggs was so graciously bestowing on him.

SONG OF THE WITCH

Sadie laughed. "I swear, if Cosmo loved you any harder he'd throw me over for you."

"Nah. He just tolerates me until you get here," Briggs said with a shrug.

Cosmo stilled and then suddenly turned over and ran to Sadie, jumping and demanding to be picked up. Sadie hauled him up into her arms, gave him snuggles, and let him lap her face with kisses.

"See." Briggs shook his head and slapped King on the shoulder. "Welcome home, brother. How long are you staying this time?"

"In Keating Hollow? A few weeks. But here?" King grimaced. "Sadie's house is finished, so we're going over there this afternoon."

"You're moving in with Sadie?" Briggs asked, looking startled.

Sadie wondered if she and Cosmo should retreat to the room that she'd been using to give them some privacy, but when King pulled her to his side, she just leaned into him.

"Yeah. I didn't mean to spring that on you, but we just decided today when Sadie got the call that the work was done," King said.

"What? No, I'm not upset." Briggs shook his head. "It's fine. It's great, actually. Congratulations. And this will give me more peace and quiet. No more moans of dissatisfaction in the middle of the night. I swear, sometimes I think you need lessons."

"What?" Sadie asked as she sputtered out a laugh.

King rolled his eyes. "Nothing. Briggs just thinks he's being funny."

"I'm being hilarious," he said and winked at Sadie. "I'm happy for you, too. But I fully expect visitation rights with that little guy." He pointed at Cosmo. "Plus, I want overnights when you guys are traveling."

Sadie grinned. "You got it."

Briggs nodded. "Now get out. I have a hot date."

"You do?" Sadie and King asked at the same time.

Briggs just flipped them off as he disappeared into his bedroom.

They both chuckled and went to pack up.

An hour later, they pulled up to Sadie's home. She grinned at the freshly painted porch, and although she'd been happy to stay at Briggs's, there was no place like home.

King busied himself with the luggage while Sadie tended to Cosmo. By the time she and her dog were done exploring the lawn, King had everything on the porch, ready to roll in.

"You're a good man to have around," Sadie said.

"I try my best." He smiled softly at her.

"Don't look at me like that," she said.

"Why?"

"Because it makes me want to rip your clothes off." She unlocked the door.

But before she could follow Cosmo in, King swept her off her feet and said, "To starting a new life together."

She stared up at him, love bursting from every molecule, and said, "I can't think of anyone I'd rather do this life with than you, King McGrath."

"Me either, Sadie Lewis. Now tell me you love me."

She giggled. "You first."

"All right," he said. "I've loved you since the first day I met you in Westhaven. And now I love you more and more every day. Sadie Lewis, will you promise to love me for the rest of your life?"

Sadie was speechless for a long moment. Then she said, "Did you just propose?"

"It sure sounded like it, didn't it?" he said, his eyes sparking with mischief.

"It did. And since I've loved you just as long, I'm saying yes. I will love you for the rest of my life. What do you say to that?"

"It sounds like someone needs to call Imogen and make an appointment." He grinned. "But how about I *show* you just how much I love you first?"

Sadie chuckled. "Have I ever told you that you have the best ideas?"

"I do, don't I?" He walked through the door, kicked it closed with one foot, and then took her to her bedroom, where he showed her not once, not twice, but three times, exactly how much he loved her.

CHAPTER 29

JANUARY

"Congratulations!" Melissa held up her champagne glass, toasting the happy couple.

The small gathering at the brewery all raised their glasses to Sadie and King. They'd just learned that their song had earned a gold record. It was the most popular song of the winter, and things could not be going better for them.

It was funny to Melissa that Sadie had turned into some sort of urban legend. After that video went viral, showing Sadie spelling those influencers, most of them had stayed away from King, believing that Sadie would hex them. It had been a blessing in disguise since King now had some sort of normalcy without being stalked all the time. And with his mother safely behind bars, their lives were about as perfect as could be.

"Cheers!" Sadie said, beaming.

Melissa had never seen her friend that happy before. She was thrilled for her. Though she did miss her. Sadie and King were gone a lot for work now, and Melissa just didn't get enough girlfriend time anymore.

Sadie saddled up to her on a barstool and said, "Man, it's been ages since we've had dinner together. Can we do that this week?"

Melissa looked over at her and wondered if she'd been reading her mind.

"What?" Sadie asked. "Are you traveling for work?"

"No. It's nothing. Yes, dinner this week. I can't wait."

Sadie gave her a sideways hug and said, "I don't know what I'd do without you."

"Same."

Her friend gave her a kiss on the cheek and hurried back over to King, who was sitting at the bar, digging into their slice of mocha caramel cheesecake.

All Melissa could do was laugh. If there was one thing that could come between her and her bestie, it was a really good piece of cheesecake.

"Hello, gorgeous," Briggs said as he took Sadie's empty seat.

"Briggs," she said coolly.

"Aww, don't be like that, Mel. I thought we were friends," he said as he looked her up and down, clearly admiring her body.

"Not that kind of friends," she reminded him.

"That's too bad, cause I think we'd be really, *really* good at being friends."

She thought so, too. The problem was Briggs was Mr. Non-Commitment. And Melissa was looking for Mr. Right, not Mr. Right Now. "Sorry, Briggs. I'm not that kind of girl anymore."

He chuckled. "My loss. Well, if you change your mind—"

"Briggs Williams, is that you?" a woman with a Southern accent called.

SONG OF THE WITCH

The man beside Melissa suddenly stiffened.

"It *is* you," the woman exclaimed. "I'd know those biceps anywhere."

Briggs glanced at Melissa and mouthed, *Help*.

She opened her mouth to respond, but before she could, Briggs wrapped an arm around her shoulders, pulled her tightly to his side, and said, "Kassie Kinny, what in the world are you doing here?"

The gorgeous petite woman with thick shiny black hair slinked up to Briggs and leaned into him. "Looking for you, of course."

"Oh," Briggs said, his eyebrows rising to his hairline. Then he cleared his throat. "Kassie, meet Melissa, my fiancée."

"Your wha—" Melissa started, but she was cut off suddenly by Briggs's mouth coming down on hers. He kissed her so thoroughly that when he finally pulled back her head was spinning.

"Well, this is a development," Kassie said, looking annoyed.

"It's new," he said sweetly and then nuzzled Melissa's ear and whispered, "Please, do me this favor."

"What are you really doing in town, Kassie?" Briggs asked.

"Oh, I wasn't lying about coming to see you," she said, glaring at Melissa. "I'm recording at Austin's studio, so you'll be mixing my tracks. I was hoping…" She placed one finger on his chest and lowered it slightly as she added, "that we could get together while I'm in town. For old times' sake."

Melissa hated the way the woman was manhandling her fake fiancée right in front of her, and without thinking, she said, "Hands off, Kassie. This guy is taken."

DEANNA'S BOOK LIST

Witches of Keating Hollow:
Soul of the Witch
Heart of the Witch
Spirit of the Witch
Dreams of the Witch
Courage of the Witch
Love of the Witch
Power of the Witch
Essence of the Witch
Muse of the Witch
Vision of the Witch
Waking of the Witch
Honor of the Witch
Promise of the Witch
Return of the Witch
Fortune of the Witch
Song of the Witch
Rise of the Witch

DEANNA'S BOOK LIST

Witches of Befana Bay:
The Witch's Silver Lining
The Witch's Secret Love
The Witch's Lost Spell

Witches of Christmas Grove:
A Witch For Mr. Holiday
A Witch For Mr. Christmas
A Witch For Mr. Winter
A Witch For Mr. Mistletoe
A Witch For Mr. Frost
A Witch For Mr. Garland

Premonition Pointe Novels:
Witching For Grace
Witching For Hope
Witching For Joy
Witching For Clarity
Witching For Moxie
Witching For Kismet

Miss Matched Midlife Dating Agency:
Star-crossed Witch
Honor-bound Witch
Outmatched Witch
Moonstruck Witch
Rainmaker Witch

Jade Calhoun Novels:
Haunted on Bourbon Street
Witches of Bourbon Street
Demons of Bourbon Street

Angels of Bourbon Street
Shadows of Bourbon Street
Incubus of Bourbon Street
Bewitched on Bourbon Street
Hexed on Bourbon Street
Dragons of Bourbon Street

Pyper Rayne Novels:
Spirits, Stilettos, and a Silver Bustier
Spirits, Rock Stars, and a Midnight Chocolate Bar
Spirits, Beignets, and a Bayou Biker Gang
Spirits, Diamonds, and a Drive-thru Daiquiri Stand
Spirits, Spells, and Wedding Bells

Ida May Chronicles:
Witched To Death
Witch, Please
Stop Your Witchin'

Crescent City Fae Novels:
Influential Magic
Irresistible Magic
Intoxicating Magic

Last Witch Standing:
Bewitched by Moonlight
Soulless at Sunset
Bloodlust By Midnight
Bitten At Daybreak

Witch Island Brides:
The Wolf's New Year Bride

The Vampire's Last Dance
The Warlock's Enchanted Kiss
The Shifter's First Bite

Destiny Novels:
Defining Destiny
Accepting Fate

Wolves of the Rising Sun:
Jace
Aiden
Luc
Craved
Silas
Darien
Wren

Black Bear Outlaws:
Cyrus
Chase
Cole

Bayou Springs Alien Mail Order Brides:
Zeke
Gunn
Echo

ABOUT THE AUTHOR

New York Times and USA Today bestselling author, Deanna Chase, is a native Californian, transplanted to the slower paced lifestyle of southeastern Louisiana. When she isn't writing, she is often goofing off with her husband in New Orleans or playing with her two shih tzu dogs. For more information and updates on newest releases visit her website at deannachase.com.

Made in United States
North Haven, CT
14 September 2025